PENGUIN BOOKS

1666

THE MISFITS

ARTHUR MILLER

The Misfits

ARTHUR MILLER

PENGUIN BOOKS

IN ASSOCIATION WITH SECKER AND WARBURG

Penguin Books Ltd, Harmondsworth, Middlesex
AUSTRALIA: Penguin Books Pty Ltd, 762 Whitehorse Road,
Mitcham, Victoria

First published in an earlier version as a short story 1957
First published in this version 1961
First published in England simultaneously in a paper-back
edition by Penguin books and in a hard-back edition by Secker
and Warburg 1961

Made and printed in Great Britain
by Cox & Wyman Ltd
London, Reading, and Fakenham

Author's Note

A GLANCE at *The Misfits* will show that it is written in an unfamiliar form, neither novel, play, nor screenplay. A word of explanation is perhaps in order.

It is a story conceived as a film, and every word is there for the purpose of telling the camera what to see and the actors what they are to say. However, it is the kind of tale which the telegraphic, diagrammatic manner of screenplay writing cannot convey because its sense depends as much on the nuances of character and place as on the plot. It therefore became necessary to do more than merely indicate what happens and to create through words the emotions which the finished film should possess. It was as though a picture were already in being, and the writer were recreating its full effects through language, so that as a result of a purely functional attempt to make a vision of a film clear to others, a film which existed as yet only in the writer's mind, there was gradually suggested a form of fiction itself, a mixed form if you will, but one which it seems to me has vigorous possibilities for reflecting contemporary existence. Movies, the most widespread form of art on earth, have willy-nilly created a particular way of seeing life, and their swift transitions, their sudden bringing together of disparate images, their effect of documentation inevitable in photography, their economy of storytelling, and their concentration on mute action have infiltrated the novel and play writing – especially the latter – without being confessed to or, at times, being consciously realized at all. *The Misfits* avowedly uses the perspectives of the film in order to create a fiction which might have the peculiar immediacy of image and the reflective possibilities of the written word.

ARTHUR MILLER

One

THERE is a permanent steel arch across Main Street bearing
a neon sign which reads WELCOME TO RENO THE BIGGEST
LITTLE CITY IN THE WORLD.

It is a quiet little town. We can see through our windshield
almost to the end of Main Street, a dozen blocks away. Everything is sharp to the eye at this altitude, the sky is immaculate,
and the morning jazz coming from the dashboard is perky. It
is a clean town. The great gambling palaces are modernistic,
battleship grey, and all their neon signs are lit in the sunshine.
The traffic light changes and our vehicle moves cautiously
ahead. But a block on we are halted by a policeman who steps
off the sidewalk, stops a truck coming the other way, and
escorts an old lady slowly across the street. She goes into the
sedate bank and trust company next to which is an elegant
women's clothing store and next to that a store with 'Craps'
in gold letters on its windows. Some stores feature 'Horse
Betting', others 'Casino', and others 'Wedding Rings'. In
this momentary halt a loud buzzing draws our attention. A
gambling emporium on the left, glistening inside, is broad-
casting the buzzing noise into the street and flashing a sign
over the sidewalk which says 'Jackpot', indicating that
somewhere within a customer has struck the full count.

The policeman, who wears gold-framed eyeglasses, waves
us on, but a woman steps up to the side window of our
vehicle. She is carrying a three-months-old baby on her arm,
and a suitcase.

The woman: 'Am I headed right for the courthouse, Mister?'

Driver's voice: 'Straight on one block and then two left.'

The woman: 'Thank you kindly. It's awfully confusin' here.'

Driver's voice: 'It sure is, ma'am.'

She steps back to the sidewalk. There is a rural pathos in her eyes, an uprooted quality in the intense mistrust with which she walks. She is thin, and her polka-dot dress is too large. She is clutching the baby and the suitcase as though she were continuously counting them.

Our vehicle moves again, keeping pace with her for a moment. The morning jazz from the dashboard remains bright and untroubled. The neon signs flash in the sunlight. The few people on the sidewalks are almost all women, and women who are alone. Many of them are strolling with the preoccupied air of the disconnected, the tourist, the divorcee who has not yet memorized the town. The jazz number ends and a hillbilly disc jockey greets his listeners. As he drawls we continue on down Main Street. Through the window of a supermarket we see a woman holding a large bag of groceries on one arm while with the other she is pulling down the arm of a slot machine; not even looking at the revolving drums, she walks away and out the door, hoping to be stopped by the crash of money which does not come. Farther on, a couple-in-love stares at bridal gowns in a store window. There is a door next to the store and a sign on it, reading 'Divorce Actions One Flight Up'. It is a prospering town with one brand-new hotel facing the Truckee River, a grey façade covered with cantilevered balconies. Beyond it rise the dry brown mountains capped with snow. One can see immense distances here, even boulders sticking out of the mountains' face. The disc jockey, in a baritone drawl, says, 'Weel, folks . . .' and for a moment there is only the sound of rustling paper coming through the radio as he evidently searches for the commercial. Two Indian young men in dungarees stand on a corner watching us pass by; their faces are like the faces of the blind, which one cannot look at too long.

The commentator chuckles. 'Folks? Here's somethin' to think about while you're a-waitin' for your vacuum-packed Rizdale Coffee to come to a boil. For the third month a-runnin', we've beat out Las Vegas. Four hundred and eleven divorces have been granted as of yesterday compared to three hundred and ninety-one for Vegas. No doubt about it, pardners, we are the Divorce Capital of the World. And speakin' of divorce, would you like to cut loose of a bad habit? How about rootin' yourself out of that chair and gettin' over to Haber's Drug Store and treat yourself to a good night's sleep with good old Dream-E-Z?'

We are going down a three-lined street, almost suburban, the houses very small, some of them frayed and nearly poor. Here is a peaceful, almost somnolent quality of a hot Nevada day. As we turn . . .

'Now naturally we don't claim to provide you with any special type of dream, friends. Dream-E-Z's only one of them names they made up back East in New York. But it does work. I can rightly swear your sleepless nights are over; you get the dream ready, and we'll give you the sleep. Dream-E-Z's a real little bottle of rest, folks, and relaxation, and peace. Put that burden down, Mother. Daddy? Let yourself go. Dream-E-Z. Come on, folks, let's get together here. . . . Say it with me now like we always do . . . all together. . . .' A school of violins soars into a music of wafting sleep. 'Dream-Eeeeee-Zeeeeee.'

The vehicle comes to a halt at the kerb and the engine is shut off and the radio with it.

Guido hops out of what we now see is a tow truck and comes around and lifts a battery out of the back. He walks up the driveway with it. The legend on the back of his jumper reads, 'Jack's Reno Garage'.

He goes behind the house, where a new Cadillac convertible stands with its hood open. The car is banged up all around, its fenders dented. He is resting the battery on the fender to get a new grip on it before lowering it into place when he hears a plane overhead. He looks up.

A great jet liner roars over, flying quite low. Guido watches it until it disappears toward the mountains, a certain longing and expert appraisal in his eyes. Then he lowers the battery into its rack and works at connecting it. He is about forty – it is hard to tell precisely because he is tanned and healthy, with close-cropped hair, strong arms, and a wrestler's way of moving his neck; from the rear he seems the athlete, even to the pigeon-toed walk and the voice that is a little too high. But face to face, talking with him, he seems to have a university-bred sophistication. Perhaps he is a football-playing poet. Then, quite suddenly, his black eyes seem to thicken into stupidity and he is a local, a naïve spender of time underneath broken cars, a man in the usual industrial daze munching his sandwich at lunch time and watching the girls go by.

Now, as he works at the battery, which is a simple job requiring only automatic fingers, his gaze spreads, and he seems to see or be longing to see something soft or something vast. The skin around his eyes and over the bridge of his nose is whiter than the rest – the mark of aviator's goggles – so that when he blinks a parrot-like look appears, the look of some heavily blinking tropical bird.

The voice of a woman turns him around.

'Young man? You have the time?'

Holding the screen door open, Isabelle shades her eyes against the morning sun. Her left arm is in a sling but she holds an alarm clock in her hand. She is a sixty-year-old tomboy with hair bobbed high in the manner of the twenties, a Buster Brown cut which somehow marks her as a woman who is impatient of details, for it rarely needs combing. She is in an old wrapper, which she holds together with her elbows. Her nose and cheeks are faintly purpled, her voice cracks and pipes, and she looks on the world with an amused untidiness that approaches an air of wreckage and a misspent intelligence. But with her first words – which cause her to cough and clear her throat – a suggestion of great kindness emerges from her. There is a cut to her speech which banishes the sentimental. She seems never to expect anything in return; she would be kind even to her executioner, perhaps apologizing for getting him up so early in the morning. For people in general she has little but despair, yet she has never met an individual she couldn't forgive. A flavour of the South sweetens her words. Seeing her, Guido feels like smiling, as most people do. She is standing there shading her eyes like an Indian as she waits to hear the time of day. He looks at his watch. As though arraigning the entire clock industry, she adds: 'I've got six or eight clocks in this house, and none of them work.'

'It's twenty after nine.'

'*After!*' Isabelle comes farther out on the porch and calls up to a second-floor window: 'Dear girl? It's twenty after!' No answer comes from the window. 'Darling?'

Roslyn appears behind the screen; we can barely make out her features. Her voice is excited as she calls down: 'Five minutes! What about you?'

'I'm all set. I just ironed my sling. The lawyer said nine-thirty sharp, darling.'

'Okay!'

Isabelle turns on hearing the car's engine start. Guido emerges from behind the wheel and stands over the engine, listening. Isabelle comes over to him, still carrying the clock which she has forgotten to set or wind.

'I hope you're not the kind to be miserly. It's brand new, you know. She ought to get a good price.'

'Is that the right mileage? Twenty-three miles?'

'We only took two rides in it. It's the damn men in this

town – they kept runnin' into her just to start a conversation.' With a proud smile: 'She's a stunner, y'know.'

Roslyn's voice: 'Will you come up here, Iz?'

'Coming, dear girl!' Then back to Guido, who is facing the upstairs window for a glimpse: 'Now you be your most generous self. You mustn't go by appearances – it's brand new, a divorce present from her husband, don't y'know.'

'They giving presents for divorces now?'

'Why not? On the anniversary of *our* divorce my husband has never failed to send me a potted yellow rose. And it'll be nineteen years July.' She is already his friend, and laughs, squeezing his arm and leaning in toward his face. 'Of course he never paid me the alimony, but I wouldn't want to put a man out anyway – if his heart's not in it, y'know.' She starts toward the porch.

'You break your arm in the car?'

'Oh, no. My last roomer before this girl – we celebrated her divorce and I . . . misbehaved. I'm just so sick and tired of myself!'

She is suddenly almost in tears and vanishes into the house. His interest piqued, Guido glances up at the window, then, taking out a pad and pencil, starts circling the car, noting down the damage.

Isabelle hurries through the house and up the stairs and goes into a room. Chaos; bureau drawers hang open; the bed is covered with letters, toilet articles, magazines, hair curlers.

From the closet, Roslyn calls: 'Could we do my answers again, Iz?'

'Oh, sure, dear.' Isabelle goes to a mirror and takes a slip of paper which is stuck in the frame. She sits on the bed, holding a pair of bent glasses to her nose. 'Let's see. "Did your husband, Mr Raymond Taber, act toward you with cruelty?"' There is no answer from the closet. 'Darling?'

After a moment: 'Well . . . yes.'

Isabelle: 'Just say yes, dear.'

A golden girl comes bursting out of the closet, zipping up her dress, and goes to the bureau, where with her free hand she searches for something in the disorder of jars, papers, and odds and ends, while glancing at her hair in the mirror. Each detail of her appearance is in perfectly good order but the total effect is windy; she can be obsessed with how she looks now, and entirely oblivious as she turns her head too quickly for her hairdo to stay in place and in a freshly pressed dress gets on her hands and knees to look under the bed for something. But quick as she is, a certain stilled inwardness lies coiled in her gaze. She glances at Isabelle.

'Yes.'

She adjusts her dress in the mirror, absorbed at the same time in the effort of answering. As with so many things she does, so many objects she examines, so many events she passes through, a part of her is totally alone, like a little child in a new school, mystified as to how it got here and passionately looking for a friendly face.

Isabelle reads on: '"In what ways did his cruelty manifest itself?"'

'He . . . How's it go again?'

'"He persistently and cruelly ignored my personal rights and wishes, and resorted on several occasions to physical violence against me."' The older woman looks up from the slip of paper.

'He persistently . . .' She breaks off, troubled. 'Must I say that? Why can't I just say he wasn't *there*? I mean, you could touch him but he wasn't there.'

'Darling child, if that was grounds for divorce there'd be about eleven marriages left in the United States. Now just repeat – '

A car horn blows. Isabelle hurries to the window. Below, Guido, putting his notepad away, speaks up to her: 'They'll call in their estimate from the office.'

Roslyn comes beside Isabelle and calls down: 'Those dents weren't my fault, you know!'

Guido now sees Roslyn for the first time, still behind the window screen, but more or less clearly. He is strangely embarrassed and ashamed of his own shyness.

'I'll recommend the best price I can, miss. You can drive her now. I put a battery in.'

'Oh, I'll never drive *that* car again. We'll call a cab.'

'I'll give you a lift in my truck if you're leavin' right away.'

'Swell! Two minutes! Get dressed, Iz! You got to be my witness!'

Isabelle grasps Roslyn's hand with a quick surge of feeling. 'This'll be my seventy-seventh time I've witnessed for a divorce. Two sevens is lucky, darlin'.'

'Oh, Iz, I hope!'

Roslyn smiles, but fear and a puzzled consternation remain in her eyes. The old lady hurries out of the room, opening the sash of her wrapper with her good hand.

Two

THERE is a small park across the street from the Reno court-house. The cross-walks are lined with benches and there is a greenish statue of a man, wife, and child facing the direction of the court – a pioneer family group to remind the litigants of the great treks that passed through here on the way West. It is a pleasant place to sit on a hot day, the shade of the tree being a rare luxury in this territory. Derelicts and old men lounge here to watch the strangers go by – sometimes young people examining proofs of their wedding pictures from the photo shop across the avenue, sometimes land claimants spreading out their maps. Anything that happens sooner or later ends up in court, and this park is where the parties can sit and stare at the issues while the traffic flows past on four sides.

Guido's tow truck pulls up. Quickly he jumps out, comes around to open the door on the other side, and helps Isabelle down.

'Easy does it, now.'

'Aren't you a dear!' Isabelle pats his shoulder.

Roslyn is almost out of the truck already, but he reaches and takes her hand, anyway. She is still clutching the slip of paper, and starts past him.

Roslyn: 'Thanks a lot. We got to run now.'

Guido gently blocks her way. 'If you're not going back East right away I'd be glad to take you out and show you the country. Some beautiful country around here, you know.'

Roslyn, distracted by her mission, thanks him with her eyes.

'I'd love to see it, but I don't know what I'm going to do yet. All I could think about here was when my six weeks would be up.'

Guido: 'Can I call you?'

'I don't know where I'll be, but okay.' Roslyn starts to move, waving back. 'Thanks again!'

Isabelle taps his arm. '*My* name is Isabelle Steers.'

Guido laughs at her jibe. 'Okay, Isabelle. You could come along if you like.'

'That's a sweet afterthought! Oh, you Reno men!' She laughs and trots after Roslyn.

Guido, somehow moved, quickened, remains staring as they walk across the paved paths that section the grass in front of the courthouse. Men on park benches look up at Roslyn as she passes; newspapers lower as she goes by.

The young polka-dot woman carrying her baby is shaking hands with a lawyer on the courthouse steps. They part. Gaunt-eyed, the woman passes Roslyn. Roslyn and Isabelle approach the steps of the court; Roslyn is rapidly going over her lines from her prompting paper. Her anxiety is hardened now.

'I can't memorize this; it's not the way it was.'

Isabelle laughs. 'You take everything so seriously, dear! Just say it: it doesn't have to be true. It's not a quiz show, it's only a court.'

They start up the courthouse steps, and as Roslyn looks up after putting her paper away she is stopped by what she sees. A man is descending the steps toward her. He is well built, tall, about thirty-eight, wearing a soft straw hat and a tie with a big design. His mind is constantly trying to tune in on the world, but the message is never clear. He feels self-conscious now, having to plead; he was successful early in life and this pleading threatens his dignity. He expects that the simple fact of his having come here will somehow convince his wife how guilty she is. But he will forgive her and she will idolize him again. He is Raymond Taber, her husband. He manages a hurt, embarrassed grin, as though confessing to a minor error he made.

'Just got off the plane. I'm not too late, am I?'

Roslyn looks at him; a rising fear for herself holds her silent. He comes down the steps to her.

'Don't, Raymond. Please, I don't want to hear anything.'

His resentment floods his face. 'Give me five minutes, will you? After two years, five minutes isn't – '

'You can't have me, so now you want me, that's all. Please ... I'm not blaming you. I never saw it any different. I just don't believe in the whole thing any more.' She starts around him and he takes her arm.

'Kid, I understand what – '

'You don't understand it, because nobody understands it!' With her finger she presses his chest. 'You aren't *there*, Raymond!' She steps back. 'If I'm going to be alone, I want to be alone by myself. Go back, Raymond – you're not going to make me sorry for you any more.'

She leaves him standing there in an impotent fury and beckons to Isabelle, who puts her arm around her. Roslyn is inwardly quaking with sobs, but she will not cry as they hurry up the steps together and into the courthouse.

Guido watches from his truck window until the two women disappear. He has seen the argument but could not hear it. Now he drives down Main Street, bemused. A train is parked across Main Street. At the crossing gate he stops, switches off the engine, and settles back in his seat to wait. His eyes show a certain fixed daze of introspection. He happens to turn and comes alert and calls out: 'Gay!'

Gay Langland is standing at the foot of the train steps with a woman. His dog is at his heels. He turns toward the truck and waves, calling: 'Wait up! I was just going over to see you!'

A conductor stands with a watch in hand a few yards off.

The woman, about forty-two, is expensively dressed. She is afraid she has been a fool and is trying to find out by searching Gay's eyes; she wears a joyless smile that is full of fear and unhappiness.

Gay is just turning back from his look at Guido. 'Good luck now, Susan. I won't forget you, you can be sure of that.'

She glances down at his proffered handclasp, and she clearly feels the formality and rejection in the gesture; she starts to shake his hand, trying to maintain composure, but suddenly she throws her arms around him and tears flood her eyes.

Gay: 'Now, now, honey, you be a good sport.'

Conductor: 'Board!'

Woman: 'I don't even know where to write you!'

Gay, reassuring her as he moves her toward the steps: 'General Delivery. I'll get it.' He gets her on to the step and she turns to him.

'Will you think about it, Gay? It's the second largest laundry in St Louis.'

'I wouldn't want to kid you, Susan. I ain't cut out for business.'

The train starts to move. The conductor hops aboard and grasps her arm to help her up. Gay walks along with the train. She has lost all her composure and is weeping.

'Will you think of me? Gay!'

'You know I will, honey! 'Bye!'

She manages a masculine, brave salute as she moves away. Even after the woman is out of sight Gay stands with his arm raised, a compassionate farewell that is full of his relief. Now he walks along the platform, the dog at his heels. Guido has pulled the truck over to the kerb; Gay comes and rests his arms on the sill of the window, and he seems weary into his voice.

'How you doin', boy? You ready to cut out of this town? 'Cause I sure am.'

'I been thinkin' about it' Guido gestures toward the

departed train; there is a certain onlooker's excitement around his eyes, a suggestive yet shy thirst for detail. 'Which one was that?'

Gay smiles at his friend's heavy curiosity, but there is a refusal to join Guido in cynicism toward her. 'Susan. Damn good sport, that woman.'

He opens the door and lets himself down on the edge of the seat. The traffic goes by quietly. Gay is forty-nine years old, a big-knuckled cowboy, a wondrous listener. He takes off his hat and wipes his sweat band. His mind is elsewhere but not in any particular place – simply not here and not now. It is the middle of a weekday morning with a stateful of sand and mountains around him. Now he seems either contented or exhausted; it is not clear which. Toward Guido he has a business friendliness, but there is no business. Maybe he has many such friends. One senses that he does not expect very much, but that he sets the rhythm for whoever he walks with because he cannot follow. And he has no desire to lead. It is always a question of arranging for the next few days, maybe two weeks; beyond that there is only the state, and he knows people all over it. Homeless, he is always home inside his shoes and jeans and shirt, and interested. When he listens, he seems to feel that life is a pageant that is sometimes loud, sometimes soft, sometimes a head-shaking absurdity, and sometimes dangerous. It is a pageant with no head and no tail. He listens, he is interested, and like a woodchuck he can go suddenly into the ground and come up later in another place. He needs no guile because has never required himself to promise anything, so his betrayals are minor and do not cling. 'If you have to you will,' he seems to believe. The moral world is full of women and he has, with their gratitude, eased many of them out of it, modestly. His refusal to mock the departed woman encourages Guido to confess his own feeling now.

Guido: 'I just met a girl sweet enough to eat, Gay. Hell of a lookin' woman.'

Gay, looking at him with pleased surprise: 'She sure must be, for you to get worked up. Look, whyn't we take out to the mountains?'

'I wanted to pile up about five hundred this time. I ought to get a new engine.'

'Hell, that engine'll fly you anywhere. You been more than two months on this job, fella – that's enough wages for one year. You gonna get the habit. I tell you, I'm just dyin' for some fresh air and no damned people, male or female. Maybe we can even do a little mustangin' up there.'

Guido looks off, indecisively. 'I'll meet you over the bar later. Let's talk about it.'

'That's the way!' Getting out, Gay slams the door shut. 'Hope I get a look at that girl!'

'Only trouble is, when I think of all the useless talkin' you gotta do I get discouraged.'

'Hell, there's nothin' more useful than talkin' to a good-looking woman. You been moody lately – might perk you up. See you later, now!'

Gay steps back, they wave to each other, and the truck takes off. Gay starts walking, a mildly revived spirit showing in his eyes.

At a certain point Main Street becomes a bridge crossing the narrow Truckee River, which flows between buildings. Roslyn and Isabelle are walking along, but Isabelle stops her at the railing. The heat of noon seems to have wilted them.

Isabelle: 'If you throw your ring in you'll never have a divorce again.'

Puzzled, Roslyn touches her ring protectively.

Isabelle: 'Go ahead, honey, everybody does it. There's more gold in that river than the Klondike.'

Roslyn, with a certain revulsion: 'Did you do it?'

Isabelle: 'Me? Oh, I lost my ring on my honeymoon!'

Roslyn: 'Let's get a drink.'

Isabelle: 'That's my girl!'

A few doors down is a casino. Open to the street, a seeming half-acre of big-chester slot machines reflect rose and blue neon light. Most of the aisles are empty now, but a few early risers are pulling at the levers, blinking in this sea of chrome, staring at glints like fish in a dim underworld. Sound is hushed here. The two women sit at a table near the bar and watch the scattered players.

A waiter comes and Roslyn orders: 'Scotch, I guess. On ice.'

Isabelle: 'Rye and water.'

The sound of well-oiled levers is peaceful in the neon gloom. The two women sit in silence for a moment, looking around. An old man nearby makes the sign of the cross over a machine and pulls the lever.

Isabelle touches her friend's arm: 'Cheer up, dear!'

'I will, I just hate to fight with anybody. Even if I win I lose. In my heart, you know?'

'Darling, you're free! Maybe the trouble is you're not used to it yet.'

'No, the trouble is I'm always back where I started. I never had anybody much, and here I – '

'Well, you had your mother, though, didn't you?'

Roslyn quells a strange feeling of shame. 'How do you have somebody who disappears all the time? Both of them weren't . . . *there*. She'd go off with a patient for three months. You know how long three months is to a kid? And he came around when his ship happened to need repairs. . . .'

The waiter comes and sets down their drinks and goes. Isabelle raises her glass. 'Well, here's to the whole damned thing, darling!'

Roslyn, suddenly grasping Isabelle's arm: 'You're a fine woman, Iz. You're practically the only woman who was ever my friend.'

'Listen! Don't leave; settle down here. There's a school

here; you could teach dancing. . . . 'Cause there's one thing about this town – it's always full of interesting strangers.' Tears show in Roslyn's eyes and Isabelle is surprised. 'Oh, my dear girl, I'm sorry; what'd I – '

'I suddenly miss my mother. Isn't that the stupidest thing?' She determinedly raises her drink, smiling. 'To . . . to life! Whatever that is.'

They laugh and drink. Roslyn sees Gay's dog sitting patiently at the foot of the bar.

Roslyn: 'Oh, look at that dear dog! How sweet it sits there!'

Isabelle: 'Yeah, dogs are nice.'

She and Isabelle see Gay placing a glass of water before the dog, Margaret. Margaret drinks. Gay glances at the two women, nods just for hello, and as he straightens up to turn back to the bar Guido enters, dressed in a clean shirt and dress trousers. Guido sees Roslyn and comes over as Gay starts to greet him.

Guido: 'Oh, hello! How'd you make out?'

Roslyn, shyly: 'Okay. It's all over.'

He nods, uncertain how to proceed, and beckons Gay over, partly as a relief for his tension.

'Like you to meet a friend of mine. This is Gay Langland. Mrs Taber . . .'

Gay, realizing she is the one: 'Oh! How-de-do.'

Guido, of Isabelle: 'And this is . . .'

'Isabelle Steers.' To Roslyn: 'One thing about Reno men, they do remember the name.'

They laugh. Isabelle is blooming. She loves new people. 'Why don't you boys sit down?'

Gay: 'Well, thank you. Sit down, Guido. Waiter? What're you girls drinkin'?'

Isabelle: 'Whisky. We're celebrating the jail burned down.'

The waitress comes to the table.

Gay: 'Get four doubles.' To Roslyn: 'You sure made a

big impression on my friend here, and' – to Guido – 'I can see why.'

Roslyn glances at Guido, but his intensity turns her to Gay and she speaks to him: 'You a mechanic too?'

Isabelle: 'Him? He's a cowboy.'

Gay, grinning: 'How'd you know?'

Isabelle: 'I can smell, can't I?'

Gay: 'You can't smell cows on me.'

Isabelle: 'I can smell the look in your face, cowboy.' She reaches across and laughs. 'But I love every miserable one of you! I had a cowboy friend. . . .' She quickly sips. 'He had one arm gone, but was more with one arm than any man with two. I mean like cooking – ' They all laugh. 'I'm serious! He could throw a whole frying-pan full of chops in the air and they'd all come down on the other side. Of course, you're all good-for-nothin', as you know.'

Gay: 'That may be, but it's better than wages.'

The waitress arrives with the drinks.

Guido: 'I suppose you're headin' back East now, huh?'

Roslyn: 'I can't make up my mind; I don't know what to do.'

Gay: 'You mean you don't have a business to run, or school to teach, or – '

'Me? I didn't even finish high school.'

'Well, that's real *good* news.'

'Why? Don't you like educated women?'

'Oh, they're all right. Always wantin' to know what you're *thinkin'*, that's all. There sure must be a load of thinkin' goin' around back East.'

'Well, maybe they're trying to get to know you better.' Roslyn smiles wryly. 'You don't mind that, do you?'

'I don't at all. But did you ever get to know a man by askin' him questions?'

'You mean, he's going to lie.'

'Well, he might not – but then again, he just might!'

25

Isabelle guffaws and the question-and-answer period gives way.

Gay: 'Let's get another drink!'

Roslyn: 'Sure, let's have some more!' His oppenness relaxes her; he is avowedly engaging her and it awakens her pleasurably.

Gay, calling to the waiter: 'Fella? See if you can get us four more, will ya?' He turns to Guido, relaxed and happy, trying to open the way. 'How about it, Pilot? We takin' out of this town today?'

Spurred, awkward, Guido falters into his campaign: 'You been out of Reno at all, Mrs Taber?'

Roslyn: 'I walked to the edge of town once, but – it looks like nothing's out there.'

Guido: 'Oh.'

Gay: 'That might just be where everything is.'

Roslyn: 'Like what?'

'The country.'

'What do you do there?'

'Just live.'

Drawn in, Roslyn searches Gay's eyes, asking: 'How can you . . . just live?'

'Well . . . you start by going to sleep. Then, you get up when you feel like it. Then you scratch yourself' – they chuckle – 'fry yourself some eggs, see what kind of day it is, throw a stone, ride a horse, visit, whistle. . . .'

Roslyn's eyes meet his. 'I know what you mean.'

Isabelle: 'Might be nice, dear, whyn't you go out for a ride?'

Guido: 'If it hit you right, I've got an empty house out in the country just beyond Hawleyville. It's yours if you want a little peace and quiet before you go back.'

Roslyn, grinning: 'Oh, is the last woman gone now?'

'No! No kidding.' With a sudden self-exposure that is difficult for Guido: 'I never offered it before.'

'Well, thanks. I wouldn't stay there, but I *was* thinking of renting a car and seeing what the country –'

'Gay's got a truck, or I could get my car.'

'No. Then you'll have to drive me back.'

'Oh, I don't mind!'

'It's all right – I always . . .' She is a little flustered at having to stand against him; she touches his hand. '. . . like to feel I'm on my own, y'know? I'll rent a car. Where can I?'

Gay: 'Right now?'

Roslyn: 'Why not?'

Gay stands up. 'Okay! You sure don't waste your time, do you?'

Guido: 'I just got to stop over at the garage and tell the boss I quit.'

Gay: 'Now, that's the boy!'

They go down an aisle of slot machines toward the street. All at once there is a goal, a path through the shapeless day.

Three

ROSLYN's rented station wagon is speeding along a straight, endless highway a quarter of a mile behind Gay's ten-year-old pickup truck. Except for the two vehicles the highway is deserted. On both sides the bare Nevada hills are spread out, range beyond range. An occasional dirt trail winding into them raises the surprising thought that one could follow it and arrive at a human place in the interior. No house shows; only an occasional line of fence indicates that cattle range here sometimes. The hills front the highway like great giants' chests; to the eye speeding past, their undulating crests rise and fall as though the earth were silently breathing. The noon sun is lighting up red woundlike stains on their surfaces, a sudden blush of purple on one, the next faintly pink, another buff. Despite the hum of the engines the land seems undisturbed in its silence, a silence that grows in the mind until it becomes a wordless voice.

Roslyn, driving with Isabelle beside her, constantly turns from the road to stare at the great round hills. Her look is inward, her eyes widened by an air of respect.

Roslyn: 'What's behind them?'

Isabelle: 'More hills.'

'What's that beautiful smell? It's like some kind of green perfume.'

'Sage, darling.'

'Oh, sure! I never smelled it except in a bottle!' Laughing: 'Oh, Isabelle, it's beautiful here, isn't it?'

Isabelle, sensing Roslyn's excitement: 'I better tell you something about cowboys, dear.'

Roslyn laughs warmly: 'You really worry about me, don't you!'

'You're too believing, dear. Cowboys are the last real men in the world, but they're as reliable as jack-rabbits.'

'But what if that's all there is? Really and truly, I mean.'

'I guess a person just doesn't want to believe that.'

'You think I'm reliable?'

'I guess you would be if you had somebody to be reliable *to*.'

'I don't know any more. Maybe you're not supposed to believe anything people say. Maybe it's not even fair to them.'

'Well . . . don't ask me, dear. This world and I have always been strangers – down deep, I mean.'

They fall silent. The hills and their colours float across Roslyn's eyes.

Up ahead, Guido is at the wheel of the truck. Beside him, Gay dozes with his hat over his eyes.

Guido: 'I couldn't hear what he said to her but' – he glances at Gay for corroboration – 'it looked like *she* left *him*. The husband.' He waits, but Gay is silent. 'She's kind of hard to figure out, y'know? One minute she looks dumb and brand new. Like a kid. But maybe he caught her knockin' around, huh?' Gay is silent. 'She sure moves, doesn't she?'

Gay: 'Yeah. She's real prime.'

Guido starts to speak again, but, glancing at Gay, decides to let him sleep. They ride in silence. They pass two Indians on brown and white paints riding slowly behind a small herd of cattle off to the right. Now Guido slows down and, sticking his head out the window, waves back at Roslyn. He turns off the highway on to a dirt trail, glancing into his mirror.

Roslyn follows in his dust across the sage flat toward the hills. In a moment they are climbing the belly of a hill. Now they are winding around behind it, rising all the time, the road becoming stony and the curves abrupt. Smashed and splintered outcroppings of rock force the trail to meander. They drive down a gap and then up a steep gorge whose flanks almost blot out the sky. Quite suddenly a house appears at the head of the gorge; Roslyn pulls up behind the truck and the motors are shut off.

She and Isabelle emerge, looking at the house. The men join them. A small cloud of buff dust slowly floats away. For a moment the sudden appearance of this vacant building enforces its silence on them.

An odd, almost other-worldly air emerges from the rather modern, ranch-style house. Its windows look out on the swiftly falling land toward the unseen highway far below and the next swell of hills rising beyond. In this vastness it seems as terribly alone as a stranded boat.

It has never been completed. Black composition sheathing panels show where the clapboards were never put on, and the boards lie in a greying, weathered pile on the ground nearby, morning glories winding through them. The gabled roof is partly shingled, but a large area is still bare to the black tar-paper underneath. Sawhorses stand in weeds and sage. An unfinished wing of bare studs and joists sticks out of one side, little sage bushes starting up through the foundation. There is an abortive look to the place, a sense of its having been immobilized by sudden catastrophe or whimsically left incomplete by people who suddenly ran away to another idea. It is not a farm or a ranch; its only visible reason for being here is that it stands at the focal point of a vast view. Yet someone rich enough to build for that reason would hardly have thought of so conventional and small a house. Its very pointlessness is somehow poetic to Roslyn, like an unrealized longing nailed together.

Roslyn: 'Why isn't it finished?'

Guido, cryptically: 'It's weather-tight. Come on in.'

Guido leads them in through the side door. He stops before

they are well inside the doorway and turns to Roslyn, patting the black insulation batting between the open studs of a partition. 'Insulated.' She nods, not quite sure what he is referring to, and he leads on into the living-room. With a wide sweep of his arm he says: 'Living-room,' and she nods, looking around at the complete assortment of furniture, from the Morris chair to the studio couch, the drapeless dirty windows, the sections of wall lined with knotty-pine boards and the sections which still show bare studs, the dusty Indian blankets on the Grand Rapids couch. The place is not damp but it seems so. Light is greyed by the dust on the windows.

Guido opens a door and presses himself against the jamb, inviting her to look out. 'This was going to be a new bedroom.'

Roslyn sticks her head into the stud skeleton of a wing built on to the house. The sun is bright in her face, and lights the ground underneath the uncovered floor joists. 'It's even nice now!'

Encouraged, Guido rushes to a series of three windows at the front of the room. 'Picture windows.'

'Oh!'

But when he arrives at the windows and looks out, the view is grey glass, and he hurries to open the front door. 'Look at that.'

With Gay and Isabelle behind her she stands in the threshold, looking out and down at the oceanic roll of mountains falling away below. 'God, it goes forever.'

'See the bathroom.' Guido touches her elbow and she follows him across the living-room. Passing the fireplace, he touches it, glancing up to where it goes through the ceiling. 'Fireplace.'

She nods. 'Brick.'

'Kitchen.'

She follows into the kitchen area, noting the spider in the sink and the damp-wrinkled box of soap flakes on the stove.

'Gas refrigerator.' He opens the freezer door and she looks in. His pride is riding him and she is drawn toward him. He closes the door and hurries through a doorway – quickly, as though he might lose her interest.

'Ceramic tile.'

In the bathroom she inspects the tile. He crosses the bathroom and opens another door and she comes up to his side.

'And here's our –' He breaks off at the sight of an ornately framed wedding photograph hanging over the bed. Two rosaries are suspended from the frame. 'My wife. She died here.'

'Oh. I'm sorry.' Roslyn glances at the barren room. A double bed, a dresser, a window, an unpainted composition-board wall. His face, and his wife's in the photograph, are curiously unmarked, new. A sadness presses in on Roslyn, and she looks at Guido's face beside her, seeing for the first time the twisting private agony behind his eyes.

Guido: 'She was due to have a baby. I was setting the capstone on the chimney, and . . . she screamed, and that was that.'

Roslyn: 'Couldn't you call the doctor?'

'She didn't seem to be that sick. Then I got a flat and didn't have a spare. Everything just happened wrong. It'll do that sometimes.'

'Oh, I know. Couldn't you live here any more?'

Guido is surprised by her flow of sympathy, and he is swept into cultivating it now. Yet one senses a fear in him of mockery, and his manner with her is tentative and delicate. 'We knew each other since we were seven years old, see.'

'You should find another girl.'

Guido, with a certain trace of vague condescension toward the idea: 'I don't know. Being with anybody else, it just seems . . . impossible, you know? She wasn't *like* other women. Stood behind me hundred per cent, uncomplaining as a tree.'

Roslyn senses an invidious comparison; she laughs lightly.

'But maybe that's what killed her.' Quickly, as she sees he feels a slur: 'I mean, a little complaining helps sometimes.' But he does not understand, and, striving for gaiety – and pardon – she takes his arm, starting him out of the room. 'Come! Show me the rest of it! It's beautiful!'

They emerge into the living-room area. Gay is sprawled on the couch; Isabelle is holding up an Indian blanket to examine it.

Roslyn: 'Isn't it beautiful here, Iz?'

Isabelle: 'It'd be perfect if somebody'd go out in the car and get the bottle of whisky I bought with my own money.'

Guido: 'Hey, that's right!' Glad for the reprieve, he jumps to the ground from the front-door threshold – there being no step.

Roslyn wanders about the room, touching things.

Gay: 'Glasses are in the kitchen, Isabelle. I'm real tired.'

Isabelle: 'No, darling, you're just a cowboy. You fellas won't get up unless it's rainin' down your neck.'

Gay laughs as the old woman goes into the kitchen area. He turns and watches Roslyn, who has halted at a dirty window to look out. He runs his eyes over her back, her legs.

'Too rough for you, Roslyn?'

A certain abstracted suspense emanates from her. 'Oh, I don't mind that.'

'Should've seen his wife. She helped pour the cement, knocked in nails. She was a real good sport.'

She looks around at the room as though trying to summon the walls' memories. 'And now she's dead. . . . Because he didn't have a spare tyre.'

'Well, that's the way it goes.'

Their eyes meet; hers resent this contradiction of her mood's truth.

'Goes the other way too, though; don't forget that.' His immovable resolution keeps her staring at him for a moment, and despite herself a vague gratitude softens her face.

Guido jumps up into the room with a small bag of groceries and a bottle. He looks at them and at Isabelle drying glasses on her sling and calls out: 'Boy, it's nice to see people in here! Come on, folks, let's get a drink.' Going to Isabelle in the kitchen area: 'I'll start the refrigerator. It makes ice quick.'

'Ice!' Isabelle calls through the open studs to Roslyn: 'We stayin' that long?'

'I don't know....'

She unwittingly looks to Gay for the decision, and he speaks to her uncertainty.

'Sure! come on, there's no better place to be! And you couldn't find better company, either!'

'All right!' Roslyn laughs.

'That's it, sport!' Gay calls to the kitchen: 'Turn on that ice, Guido boy!'

Isabelle comes in, balancing a tray and glasses, which Gay leaps up to take – along with the bottle from her sling. Gay pours.

Gay: 'Let's get this stuff a-flowin' and make the desert bloom.'

Isabelle: 'Flow it slow. We only got the one bottle.'

Gay grasps Roslyn's wrist and puts the glass into her hand. 'There you are, now! Put that in your thoughts and see how you come out.'

She smiles at him, warmed by his persistence.

Guido enters and takes a glass. 'Come on, sit down, every-body! Let's get comfortable.'

Roslyn sits on the couch, Isabelle beside her. The two men take chairs.

Guido addresses Roslyn, his hope flying: 'Say, I'm really glad you like this place.'

Isabelle: 'Well, here's to Nevada, the leave-it state.'

Roslyn: 'The what state?'

They are already starting to chuckle.

'The leave-it state. You want to gamble your money,

leave it here. A wife to get rid of? Get rid of her here. Extra atom bomb you don't need? Just blow it up here and nobody will mind in the slightest. The slogan of Nevada is, "Anything goes, but don't complain if it went!"'

Gay: 'God, that's no lie!'

Guido: 'How come you never went back home, Isabelle? You came out here for your divorce, didn't you? Originally?'

Isabelle drinks, glances diffidently at Roslyn. 'Tell you the truth, I wasn't beautiful enough to go home.'

Roslyn: 'Oh, Isabelle!'

'It's true, darling. Beauty helps anywhere, but in Virginia it's a necessity. You practically need it for a driver's licence. I love Nevada. Why, they don't even have mealtimes here. I never met so many people didn't own a watch. Might have two wives at the same time, but no watch. Bless 'em all!'

Roslyn, relaxing, is leaning her head back on the couch as they drink. Their rhythm has slowed. Their laughter slides away now.

Roslyn: 'How quiet it is here!'

Sprawled out, Gay speaks with avowed seriousness. 'Sweetest sound there is.'

They sip their drinks. There is a skylike silence in the room.

Guido: 'There's an Indian store about five miles' – Roslyn looks at him quizzically – 'if you wanted to shop. Groceries, everything. If you decided to stay a while.'

Gay, plainly, without any insinuation: 'Be glad to come by and do your chores. If you liked.'

Roslyn drinks again and gets up. They watch as, in a closed world of her own, she wanders to a half-empty bookcase. Unable to bear the silence she turns to the men. 'Could we have a fire?'

Guido: 'Sure! It's a good fireplace.' He springs up and piles wood into the fireplace. He looks up at her, dares to smile, thankful for her command.

She smiles back abstractedly and, turning from Guido, sees that Gay has been watching the silent exchange. She smiles at Gay and he replies with a frankly intensified gaze at her. She says to Isabelle: 'Maybe they know your friend.' To the men: 'You ever know a fellow named Andy?'

Gay: 'Andy who?'

Isabelle: 'Stop it, darling! You can't go lookin' for a man.'

Gay: 'What'd he, take off?'

'Not exactly. He just didn't come back.' Isabelle laughs at herself. 'Andy Powell? You ever –'

'Sure! Fella with one arm. Call him Andy Gump sometimes?'

Isabelle, a little excited in spite of herself, laughing: 'That's him!'

Roslyn, hopefully for Isabelle, asks Gay: 'Where is he?'

'Saw him at the rodeo only last month.'

Roslyn: 'Could you find him if you –'

Isabelle: 'Dear girl, you got to stop thinkin' you can change things.'

A mystifying flood of protest reddens Roslyn's face. 'But if there's something you could do . . . *I* don't know what to *do*, but if I knew, I'd do it!'

She suddenly finds the three of them looking at her in silence, looking at her as though she had challenged them in some secret way. Gay's interest is heightened; Isabelle feels a little ashamed and ineffectual; Guido is vaguely frightened by this burst of feeling and drawn to her. Because there is no one here to receive her meaning as she intends it, she says, almost laughing: 'Is there a phonograph or a radio? Let's get some music.'

Guido: 'There's no electricity.'

Roslyn: 'How about the car radio?'

Gay: 'Now who'd've thought of that? Turn it on, Guido!'

Guido: 'You always got an idea, don't you.' Excitedly he rushes out, hopping down to the ground.

Gay: 'How about another drink, Roslyn? It'll keep the first one warm.'

Roslyn: 'I'd love it.'

The car engine is heard starting outside. With strangely youthful energy Isabelle gets up and heads for the kitchen. 'Think I'll make a sandwich. How about you people?'

Roslyn: 'Okay.'

Isabelle goes into the kitchen area. Gay, close to Roslyn, pours a drink into her glass and says in a private tone: 'I hope you're going to stay on here. Any chance?'

Her face fills with a sadness that approaches a strange self-abandonment. 'Why? What difference would it make?'

'Might make all the difference in the world as time goes by.'

She looks at him with the unconcealed intensity of a searcher, and he does not evade it. Jazz is heard from the car radio outside. The engine is shut off. Gay touches her arm. 'Like to dance?'

'Okay.'

He draws her to him. He is a fair dancer. Guido enters, and is rather caught in mid air by this progress.

Roslyn calls over Gay's shoulder to Guido: 'Thanks! Iz, give him another drink. It's a very nice house, Guido.'

Isabelle comes out of the kitchen area. Guido goes around them and forces an interest in stoking up the fire. In his face, seen in the firelight, there is rapid, planning thought.

Isabelle, making sandwiches with one hand: 'That's pretty good dancing cowboy!'

Gay: 'Hey, what're you makin' my feet do?'

Roslyn is getting quite high; her body is moving more freely. 'Relax. Join your partner, don't fight her.'

'*I* ain't fightin' her.'

She breaks and tries to move him into a Lindy. He does it awkwardly, but amazed at himself.

Guido: 'What *are* you doin'?'

Guido and Isabelle are watching with intrigued smiles.

Guido drinks deeply now, a competitive tension rising in him. Isabelle speaks with quiet pride to Guido: 'She taught dancing y'know, before she was married.'

'No kiddin'! In a dance hall?'

'Something like that, I guess.'

The information tends to place Roslyn for Guido. Suddenly he breaks in between her and Gay. 'How about the landlord?' Lightly, to Gay: 'Move over, boy, huh?'

'Just watch out for those pretty little feet there!'

Guido looks directly at Roslyn, his eyes firing, an almost ludicrous familiarity in his grin. 'Oh, she knows how to get out of the way. Let's go!'

With a clap of his hands, he astounds them all by breaking into a boogie Lindy. Roslyn immediately, and happily, accepts the challenge. They come together, part, dance back to back, and he puts her to her mettle.

Gay: 'Where in hell you learn that, Pilot?' To Isabelle: 'I never knew him to dance at all!' Calling: 'Look at Pilot comin' out from under the bushel!'

The number ends, and on the last beat Guido has her pressed close, and in the silence she deftly, but definitely – smiling, however – breaks his grip on her body, her expression striving to deny the easy victory in his eyes.

Gay: 'You two oughta put on a show! That's some goin', Roslyn!'

Roslyn: 'Whew!' Panting, getting high, she staggers to the door. Another number starts from the radio. Guido goes to her, clasps her waist, and turns her around to him familiarly. 'Come on, honey, this is a good one. I haven't danced in years.' They dance with quicker knowledge of each other now. After a moment she asks: 'Didn't your wife dance?'

'Not like you. She had no . . . gracefulness.'

Roslyn stays close to him and looks up into his face: 'Whyn't you *teach* her to be graceful?'

'You can't learn that.'

38

'How do you know? I mean, how do you *know*?'

Guido is stumped by her veering thought. Resentment mars his face.

Roslyn: 'You see? She died, and she never knew how you could dance! It's nobody's fault, but to a certain extent' – she holds thumb and index finger a half-inch apart – 'I mean just to a certain extent maybe you were strangers.'

Guido, injured, his tone on the verge of contempt: 'I don't feel like discussing my wife.' He stops dancing.

Roslyn takes his arm. The jazz is going, she is high now, and a depth of sadness comes over her face. 'Oh, don't be mad! I just meant that if you loved her you could have taught her anything. Because we have to die, we're really dying right now, aren't we? All the husbands and all the wives are dying every minute, and they are not teaching one another what they really know.' She sees he is at a loss and genuinely tries to plead with him. 'You're such a nice man, Guido.' She wipes her hair out of her eyes to blot out the sight of his resentful face, and suddenly: 'I want air!'

Turning quickly to the front door she starts to step out. Gay rushes from the couch and catches her before she goes down where the step is missing. Isabelle rushes right behind him.

Gay: 'You better lie down, girl.'

Isabelle: 'Come on, let's get back home. Heist her down, cowboy.'

Roslyn: 'No, I'm all right, I'm all – '

She starts once again to walk out the door. Guido leaps down to the ground and she falls into his arms, standing up. She is looking into his face, laughing in surprise at her sudden drop, when he thrusts his lips against hers, squeezing her body to him. She pushes him away.

Above them on the threshold Isabelle calls with fear in her voice: 'Help me down! Get in the car, Roslyn!'

Roslyn sends Guido falling a step back and staggers away.

Momentarily alone, she looks around her. The radio jazz is still playing. She flies into a warm, longing solo dance among the weeds, and coming to a great tree she halts and then embraces it, pressing her face against its trunk.

Guido, Isabelle, and Gay are watching now in a group at the doorway of the house, mystification on their faces. Guido, still resentful, takes a step toward her, but Gay touches him and he stops. Gay goes through the weeds to the tree and gently tries to turn Roslyn's shoulder, for her face is hidden under her arm. As soon as he touches her she turns and faces him and, astonishingly, her face is bright and laughing. Gay starts to smile, but he is bewildered.

Roslyn: 'You were worried about me! That's so sweet!'

Gay: 'Just want to keep you in one pretty piece.'

He puts his arm around her and she lets herself be led to her station wagon, which is parked beside Gay's beat-up pickup truck. At the car's open door, Gay turns to Guido and begins to speak, but Guido cuts him off: 'Go ahead, you drive her, I'll take your truck.'

Gay moves Roslyn into the car, and she says: 'No, don't leave Guido all alone. Go ahead, Iz. . . . Ride with poor Guido.' In apology she reaches toward Guido: 'It's a beautiful house, Guido!'

Gay gets in beside her.

Both vehicles descend the rocky trail to the highway below, the truck ahead. Inside the station wagon, Roslyn is sitting beside Gay, one leg tucked under, her foot almost touching Gay's hip. She is in the momentary calm after a quick storm, blurred eyes staring out at the passing hills that rise from the roadside. She turns to look at Gay's profile; a calm seems to exude from him, an absence of uncertainty which has the quality of kindness, a serious concern for which she is grateful. She speaks: 'I didn't mean to hurt his feelings. Did I hurts his feelings?'

Gay, grinning: 'You sure brought out the little devil in

him – surprised me.' He laughs. 'He did look comical doin'
that dance!' He guffaws.

They have arrived at the foot of the trail. The truck has
entered the highway, turned, and moved off. Now Gay stops
the car, he looks left and right for traffic, and his eyes fall on
Roslyn; she is looking at him searchingly, a residual smile
lingering on her face.

'You're a real beautiful woman. It's ... almost kind of
an honour sittin' next to you. You just shine in my eyes.' She
laughs softly, surprised. 'That's my true feeling, Roslyn.' He
pulls up the brake, shifts around to face her. 'What makes you
so sad? I think you're the saddest girl I ever met.'

'You're the first man ever said that. I'm usually told how
happy I am.'

'You make a man *feel* happy, that's why.'

He tries to embrace her; she gently stops him. 'I don't feel
that way about you, Gay.'

Gay, pleased, somehow, holds up her chin. 'Well, don't
get discouraged, girl – you might! Look, whyn't you try it out
here a while? You know, sometimes if a person don't know
what to do, the best thing is to just stand still ... and I
guarantee you'd have something out here you wouldn't find
on every corner.'

She asks him with her eyes.

'I may not amount to much some ways, but I am a good
friend.'

Roslyn, touching his hand: 'Thanks.'

Gay, encouraged, quickly puts the car in gear: 'Let me
take you back, and you get your things. . . .' He drives on to
the highway with heightened urgency. 'Try it for a week, see
what happens.' They drive for a moment. 'You ever hear the
story of the city man out in the country? And he sees this
farmer sittin' on his porch, and he says, "Mister, do you know
how I can get back to town?" And the fella says, "Nope."
And the city man says, "Well can you tell me how to get to

the post office? And the fella says, "Nope." "Well, do you know how to get to the railroad station?" "Nope." "Mister," he says, "you sure don't know much, do you?" And the farmer on the porch says, "Nope. But I ain't lost."'

They laugh together. A certain reserve dissolves in her, as she senses a delicacy in his feeling, an unwavering attention on her. Even when he turns away she feels herself in the centre of his gaze.

She asks: 'Don't you have a home?'

'Sure. Never was a better one, either.'

'Where is it?'

'Right here.'

With a gesture of his head he indicates the open country. She looks out the window for a house on the moonlit land, but seeing only the deserted hills she again faces his profile, drawn by his self-containment. She turns back to the night outside, trying to touch a point of rest in the vastness there.

Four

THE end of night. Stars recede and go out, the sun's rim appears above the sea of hills, and the sky swiftly catches fire, sucking the vision of the eye toward the circular horizon and an earth in peace. Bird songs as clear as the air whistle the sun back into the sky. The eye tires of distances and seeks detail, and rapacity emerges; a rabbit hops from under a sage bush and a shadow passes over it. A hawk, serene, floats in narrowing circles above. The bird songs become jagged and strident. Swallows from nowhere dive at the soaring hunter to drive him off. A butterfly lights on a stone and a chameleon's tongue flicks out and takes it.

The sunlight moves into the bedroom of Guido's house, where Roslyn is asleep. The screaming of the birds seems to be penetrating her dreams; her face tenses and one fist begins to close. The empty pillow beside her head is dented.

The door to the living-room opens and Gay stands there looking down at her, his gaze fingering the outlines of her body under the sheet. The picture of Guido and his wife is gone from over the bed, only the hook remaining. There is desire in Gay's face and the scent of her body still clings to his, but his eyes are searching as though through a mist emanating from her. Some wonder has taken place and is still unfolding itself within him, an unforetold consequence of pleasure. Unconsciously he smooths his hair back and in the gesture is a worry that he is not quite young any more.

She stirs under his stare and now opens her eyes, and he

comes and knee-bends beside the bed. As her eyes open he leans in and kisses her. She seems for a moment not to know where she is. Then she smiles, and her eyes look around the room and she stretches. 'Boy, I'm hungry!'

'Come on out, I got a surprise.'

He walks out of the room. She sits up, her face showing a pleasurable anticipation, and she starts out of bed.

Gay goes to the stove and turns over some eggs in a pan. Near him is a kitchen table set for two. He turns and sees Roslyn in a terry-cloth robe emerging from the bedroom doorway.

She looks about in surprise. 'You been *cleaning?*'

She moves, sees the table set, the breakfast sizzling on the stove, and in a vase a few wild flowers. Something outside the door catches her eyes. She looks and sees a mop standing in an empty pail among the weeds. Now she turns to him. She is moved by this effort. She hurries toward him at the stove. 'Here, let me cook.'

'Just sit down, it's all done.'

He dishes out eggs for both of them and sits opposite her. She stares at him. He starts eating.

'You always do this?'

'Uh-uh. First time for me.'

'Really and truly?'

Gay nods; his having gone out of himself is enough.

She starts eating. 'Oooo! It's delicious!'

She eats ravenously. He watches with enjoyment. 'You really go all out, don't you? Even the way you eat. I like that. Women generally pick.'

In reply she smiles and returns to eating, and it joins them for a moment. Now she looks up at him and says with a full mouth: 'The air makes you hungry, doesn't it?'

He laughs softly. Now he is sipping his coffee. He lights a cigarette, always trying to sound her.

She eats like one who has starved. Now she stops for a

breath. 'I love to eat!' Happily she looks around the room. 'I'd never know it was the same house. It even smells different.'

Suddenly she goes around the table and kisses his cheek. 'You like me, huh?'

He draws her down to his lap, kisses her on the mouth, holds her with his head buried in her. She pats his neck, an uneasiness rising into her face mixed with her happiness. He relaxes his hold. She gets up, walks to the doorway, looks out at the endless hills, the horizon, the empty sky.

'Birds must be brave to live out here. Especially at night.' She turns to him, explaining. 'Whereas they're so small, you know?'

'M-m.'

Roslyn, almost laughing: 'You think I'm crazy?'

'Uh-uh. I just look that way 'cause I can't make you out.'

'Why?'

'I don't know. . . . You got children?'

She shakes her head. Some embarrassment seems to have risen in her at the question; she turns out again, and seeing a butterfly lighting on the threshold, does a knee-bend and holds out her finger toward it but it flies off. She spreads out on her stomach with her head in the doorway. Now she glances back at him and decides to answer him.

'I didn't want children. Not with him.'

'He did, though, huh?'

'Children supposedly bring you together. But what if they don't, you know? Because I've known couples, so-called happily married, and one time' – she turns to him, rolling on to her side – 'the wife was actually in the hospital to have the baby and he was calling me up. I mean *calling me up*. And they're still supposed to be happily married.'

'I guess you believe in true love, don't you?'

'I don't know, but somebody ought to invent where you can't have kids unless you love each other. Because kids know the difference. I always knew.' Suddenly, even cheerfully: 'If you want to go anywhere I don't mind being alone.'

Gay comes over to her and knee-bends beside her, runs his fingers through her hair. 'I look like I want to leave?'

'I just want you to do what you feel like.'

'I never saw anything like it.'

'What?'

'You ain't kiddin'. Even when you're kiddin', you ain't kiddin'.'

She laughs. 'Most people don't like it.'

'Makes me feel peaceful.' He sits on the floor. For a moment they are silent. 'You know, they come here from New York, Chicago, St Louis – and find them a cowboy. Cowboy's supposed to be dumb, y'know, so they'll tell him everything. And they'll do everything, everything they couldn't do back home. And it's pitiful.'

'Why is it pitiful?'

'Cowboy's laughin' at them and they don't know it. Sure is nice to meet somebody who's got respect for a man.'

'You ever think of getting married again?'

'Oh, I've thought of it lots of times, but never in daylight.'

She laughs easily, recognizing his nature, and he grins in admission of it.

He comes to a complete stillness, and whatever strategic quality structured their questions and answers falls away. His direct, unwavering gaze awakens a wisp of fear in her. 'I'll tell you this, though. I wouldn't know how to say good-bye to you, Roslyn. It surprises me.'

The silence suddenly seems like an onrushing wave that will smother her. She reaches thankfully for his hand, but her eyes are growing distant, protecting her.

He looks around at the room. 'There'd be a lot to do around this place if you were going to stay a while.'

She is on her feet, drawing him up by the hand. 'Let's go in the sun!'

They drop down to the ground from the threshold and walk through the weeds reflectively, hand in hand.

'You got respect for a man. I can't stand these women all the time sayin' what they would do and what they wouldn't do.'

She laughs.

'And they go and do it anyway.'

They sit on the lumber pile. She looks up at the blue, cloudless sky. 'I really make you peaceful?'

He nods. 'I sure wish I knew whether you were stayin' or goin'.'

She bends to a pebble and cleans the dirt off it. 'When I know myself I'll tell you. Okay? Let's just live – like you said in the bar?' Apologetically, with almost a laugh: 'I don't know where I am yet – you know?'

She gets off the lumber and her eye happens to fall on a cement block in the weeds. Grateful for even this small escape, she almost dances over to it. 'Look! Couldn't we use this for a step?'

He walks over and picks up the block. 'Just might at that.' He goes the few yards to the front door and sets the block under it. 'There now!'

'Let me try it.' She hurries and runs up the step into the house, then turns and hops down. 'It's perfect! I can come in and I can go out.' Again she jumps up into the house and out again, and her pure enthusiasm moves him, and he laughs with the surprise of a youth. She senses his naïve, genuine feeling, and with sudden gratitude and hope cries out: 'Oh, you're a dear man, Gay!' He kisses her speaking mouth as she once more comes dancing out of the doorway.

Five

THERE were weeds around the house, hunks of dried cement, and scabs of bare ground. Now Gay is hoeing in a new vegetable garden nearby and flowers have been planted around the rocks, a fallen fence has been repaired, and a hose is spouting water over new grass. Sweat is dripping from his chin as he works the hoe around young vegetable plants. A deep hum in the sky raises his head. The sound grows. He turns in a circle.

Roslyn appears in the doorway, then comes down toward him, carrying a pitcher of lemonade and a glass. The roar is descending on them, and as she reaches him a small biplane zooms over the ridge of the house, waggling its wings. Gay yells: 'Guido!' and waves. The plane swings around in a curve over the falling valley and she waves with him. It disappears.

Roslyn: 'Where's he going?'

Gay: 'Sssh!' He listens. She is puzzled. 'He might be gonna land back there. There's a place.' They listen. Silence. 'I guess not. Probably just sayin' hello.'

'Here have some lemonade.'

'Thanks.' He takes it and drinks and she sits on a stone.

'What does he do, just fly around?'

He hands back the glass and picks a splinter out of his palm. 'He might be goin' for eagles. Now and again the ranchers hire Guido to shoot eagles.'

'Why?'

'They kill a lot of lambs. He gets fifty bucks a bird. It's nice work.'

'Why doesn't he ever come around? I hope he's not mad at me.'

'Oh, no. Women don't mean too much to Guido. He's probably been layin' around readin' his comic books, that's all.'

He works the ground again. Squatting on the stone, she seems to join the sun and the earth in staring at him, watching his hoe awakening the soil around the plants. He senses an importance for her in his expertness, and he winks down at her.

She smiles and breaks her stare. 'I like you, Gay.'

'That's good news.'

'You like me?'

'Well, it's close to ninety degrees out here, and I'm hoein' a garden for the first time since I was ten years old, so I guess I must like you pretty good.'

She reaches out and touches a plant. 'I never really saw anything grow before. How tiny those seeds were – and still they know they're supposed to be lettuces!'

'You say the damnedest things, you know that?'

They laugh quietly. He works the ground. She looks off now at the distant hills. She is almost content; she knows she might well be content but something gnaws at her, and she listens to it.

'In Chicago everybody's busy.'

He glances at her; he doesn't quite understand what she means, but the feeling is a welcoming one, so he lets it go.

'You ever get lonesome for your children?'

For a moment he works in silence; it might be reticence or a bad recollection. She starts to change the subject but he speaks.

'I see them couple of times a year. They come whenever I'm in a rodeo. I'm a roper.' He works for a moment, bends, and tosses a rock out of the garden. 'I do get lonesome. Sure.'

'They must like you.'

'I guess they do. My daughter's almost your size now. You size twelve?'

'Uh-huh.'

'So's she. I bought her a dress for Christmas. Size twelve.'

Effortlessly she jumps up and goes to him; her movement is imperative and surprises him. She embraces him and kisses him passionately. Her face is very serious, nearly in pain. He lets the hoe drop from his hand. Roslyn sees he is puzzled. 'Go ahead. Work.' She returns to the stone and sits. He resumes hoeing. 'What happened; you just stop loving your wife?'

He speaks out of vivid memory and it is discomfiting to go into. 'Well . . . I come home one night and find her wrapped up in a car with a fella. Turned out to be one of my real old friends, too. Cousin of mine, matter of fact.'

'Huh! And you didn't have any idea, before?'

The intensity of a blush tightens his eyes.

'God, no! In those days I thought you got married, and that was it. But nothin's it. Not forever.'

'That's what I could never get used to – everything's always changing, isn't it?'

Gay rests on the hoe, looking down at her. 'You been fooled an awful lot, haven't you?'

With a certain shame that is without self-pity, she whispers: 'Yes.'

'Well, let's just see if it turns out different this time. You're not going anywhere?'

'I'm here.'

'Well, let's leave it that way for now. Okay?'

'How dear you are! You didn't get mad at me.'

She kisses him again quickly, then, filled with an unspeakable relief, a sense of somehow having been pardoned and accepted, she clasps her hands together with her face toward the sky, her whole body on tiptoe. 'I love this whole state!'

She laughs at herself and he grins in surprise. She picks up his hoe and hands it to him as though to keep the present image of him from vanishing. 'Here. I love to see a man working around his house.'

But his eye has caught something on the ground. He bends to a plant. 'Now what have we here?'

He unfolds the leaves of a nibbled lettuce. Now he turns about and sees several more damaged plants farther up the row. He scans the brushy borders of the garden.

'It's plain old rabbit, and I'm gonna get him!' He drops his hoe and starts toward his truck beside the house, calling, 'Margaret! Come here now!'

The dog appears around a corner, alert and eager. Gay goes to his truck and takes a shotgun out from behind the seat, then a handful of shells. He is loading the gun when Roslyn comes to him, still carrying the lemonade pitcher. She is trying to appear smiling, but her anxiety is clear.

'Maybe they won't eat any more.'

Gay, busy with his gun, eager for the kill, speaks rapidly of what he knows: 'No, ma'am. Once they zeroed in on that garden it's them or us. There won't be a thing left by the end of the week.'

He starts past her with his gun. She touches his arm. She is trying to suppress her anxiety and it thins her voice. 'Couldn't we wait another day and see? I can't stand to kill anything, Gay.'

'Honey, it's only a rabbit.'

'But it's alive, and . . . it doesn't know any better, does it?'

'Now you just go in the house and let me –'

She graps his arm and her adamance astounds him. 'Please, Gay! I know how hard you worked –'

'Damn right I worked hard!' He points angrily at the garden and tries to laugh. 'I never done that in my life for anybody! And I didn't do it for some bug-eyed rabbit!'

He takes off toward the garden, the eager dog at his heel. She tries to turn back to the house, but is driven to follow him.

A little breathless now, with the ice-filled lemonade pitcher still clinking in her hand: 'Gay, please listen.'

Gay turns on her now, smiling, but his eyes full of anger. 'You go into the house now and stop bein' silly!'

'I am not silly!'

He starts off again, she calls: 'You have no respect for me!'

Gay turns, suddenly furious, red-faced.

She pleads now: 'Gay, I don't care about the lettuce!'

'Well, *I* care about it! How about some respect for me?'

A sound from behind the house turns them both. Gay walks a few steps toward one corner, when, from a trail that climbs the hill behind the house, Guido appears, helping Isabelle along. She is no longer wearing a sling, but her arm is still bandaged.

Roslyn runs toward her with high relief and joy, 'Isabelle, Guido, how are you?'

Isabelle: 'Dear girl!'

The women embrace. Gay comes and shakes Guido's hands, happy at this visit. 'How you been, fella? We never heard you land.'

Isabelle holds Roslyn before her. 'My, you look thrivin'!'

Guido has been glancing at the place, and now walks to get a better vantage. 'Am I in the right place?' His voice cracks into a giggle.

Roslyn is extraordinarily sympathetic toward him, and Guido, despite the conventionality of his remarks, is moved by what he sees.

'Did you see the vegetable garden?' Roslyn turns to draw in Gay and even to give him pre-eminence. 'Gay did it. Took him a whole week just to get the soil turned over.'

Gay walks up beside her, and now that her feeling for him has returned he puts an arm around her waist. With wry pride: 'Mowed the grass and put in them flowers, too. Even got your windows unstuck, and your fireplace don't smoke any more.'

Guido turns from Gay to Roslyn. There is a subtle resentment toward both of them, but at the same time his eyes seem charged with a vision beyond them. 'Roslyn, you must be a magician. The only thing this boy ever did for a woman was to get out the ice cubes.'

They all laugh, trying to obliterate his evident uneasiness.

Roslyn, pointing to the outdoor furniture and taking Guido's arm: 'We got chairs! Come, sit down!'

Gay intercepts them. 'Let's show him the inside. Wait'll you see this, Guido! I've moved that furniture around so many times I'm gettin' long ears.'

He and Guido move together toward the doorway. Roslyn and Isabelle follow behind. The men go into the house.

Isabelle: 'Darling, you look so lovely! You found yourself, haven't you?'

Roslyn tries to dispel her own hesitation and ends by hugging Isabelle. 'I'm so glad you came! Look, we have a step now.'

She helps Isabelle into the house, Isabelle giving a marvelling look at the flower bed beside the step as she mounts up.

'Watch your arm – how is it?'

'It's still weak as a bird's wing, but –' Entering the living-room, she breaks off. 'Well, I never in my life . . .'

Guido and Isabelle look at each detail in the room. Indian blankets cover the formerly bare studs; wild flowers brighten the tables and window sills; the furniture is rearranged, cleaned; the newly curtained windows are no longer smeared with dust and cobwebs; and the fireplace is all white. There is a feeling here of a shelter.

Tears flow into Isabelle's eyes. 'Well! Huh! My – it's magical!' She looks at Roslyn, then she addresses Gay, almost rebuking him. 'I just hope you know that you have finally come in contact with a real woman.' She suddenly throws her arms around Roslyn. 'Oh, my darling girl!'

'Come, see the bedroom. Come, Guido.' Roslyn pulls them

both to the bedroom. 'I hope you don't mind we changed things around. . . .'

Gay, with an excitement previously unknown to him, opens the refrigerator and takes out cubes. Roslyn, Guido, and Isabelle enter the bedroom; it too is transformed, re-painted, brightly curtained, with a carpet on the floor, a few botanical pictures on the walls, a dressing-table, a bright spread on the bed. Guido looks about and his eyes fall on the place above the bed where the picture of himself and his dead wife had been. A print of a Western landscape hangs there now.

Roslyn sees the direction of his gaze. 'Oh! I put your picture in the living-room!'

'Uh-huh. Put a closet in?'

'Gay did it.'

She swings the door of the closet open to show him. Inside the door half a dozen photos of her are tacked up. They are girlie photos for the doorway of a second-class nightclub, herself in net tights, on her back, in bizarre costumes. She realizes only now, partly by the flush on his face as he sees the photos, that she has shown them to him.

'Oh, they're stupid, don't look at them!' She closes the door. He looks embarrassed for her, perplexed. 'Gay put them up for a joke. Come. Let's have a lot of drinks!'

She shepherds them into the living-room and goes on to the kitchen to spread crackers around a piece of cheese on a platter. Gay is coming to them with drinks.

Guido's face is flushed as he strives against his envy. 'Man, you sure got it made this time.'

Roslyn calls from the kitchen area with high joy: 'Sit down, everybody. I got wonderful cheese. It's so nice to have company!' They are dispersing to the couch and chairs, but she rushes to Guido, who is about to sit on the couch. 'No! Sit in the big chair.' Leading him – he is embarrassed – to the most imposing chair in the room: 'This must have been your chair, wasn't it?'

'Matter of fact it was. I did all my studying in this chair. When I was still ambitious.' He sits stiffly, like one who feels vaguely threatened at being served.

She rushes back to the kitchen area. 'Maybe you'll get ambitious again, you can't tell. I'll get you some cheese.' She gets the cheese tray from the kitchen counter and, returning to Guido, points with it toward his wedding photograph on a table. 'I put your picture there – is that all right?'

'Oh, you don't have to keep it out, Roslyn.'

'Why? It's part of the house, Guido. Y'know?' She sets the tray down and sits beside Gay on the couch, taking a drink from the table where he set it for her. Now they are settled. 'I mean, it's still your house. Here, Isabelle, rest your arm on this.' She leaps up with a cushion from the couch and sets it under Isabelle's bandaged arm.

'Oh, don't bother with me, dear.'

'Why? Might as well be comfortable.'

Roslyn goes back to the couch and sits beside Gay, as Guido speaks. His voice is suddenly portentous. 'I'm going to tell you something, Roslyn.' With a strained, self-deprecating grin that lowers a driving pressure on to his words: 'I hope you don't mind, Gay, because I love this girl, and you might as well know it.'

Putting a proprietary arm loosely around Roslyn's shoulders, Gay grins. 'Well, you'd be out of your head if you didn't.'

Guido faces Roslyn. A formality sets in that is faintly self-pitiful and oddly dangerous. 'I spent four years in the war: two tours. Fifty missions. And every time I came back to base I started to design this house. But somehow I could never get it to look like my idea of it. And now it almost does. You just walk in, a stranger out of nowhere, and for the first time it all lights up. And I'm sure you know why, too.'

Roslyn, her voice faint in the face of his curiously intense feeling: 'Why?'

'Because you have the gift of life, Roslyn. You really want to live, don't you?'

His remorseless sincerity silences the room.

Roslyn: 'Doesn't everybody?'

Guido glances at the picture. 'No, I think most of us . . . are just looking for a place to hide and watch it all go by.'

Isabelle: 'Amen!'

Guido, raising his glass, persisting in his formality: 'Here's to your life, Roslyn – I hope it goes on forever.'

She quickly reaches over and clicks her glass with his. 'And yours. And yours, Isabelle.' And with the faintest air of an afterthought: 'And yours, Gay.'

We notice the slightest flicker in Gay, an awareness that he has been placed slightly to one side. They drink.

Roslyn moves closer to Gay. 'Gay did all the work, you know.'

'Yeah, and the rabbits are really enjoyin' it, too.' He grins, and only now puts his arm around her.

Guido sees the reconciliation of a conflict in them and he feigns ignorance, but there is condescension in his question: 'You think you could break away from paradise long enough to do some mustangin'?'

'Mustangin'!' Gay's look sharpens. 'Now you're sayin' something. You been up to the mountains?'

'I took a quick look up there this morning. Spotted fifteen horses.'

'That's not bad. I'd sure like to lay my hand on a rope again. What do you say?'

Isabelle turns to Roslyn, shaking her head. 'I will never understand cowboys. All crazy about animals, but the minute they got nothin' to do they go runnin' up the mountains to bother those poor wild horses.' Passionlessly, to the men: 'Shame on you!'

Roslyn: 'Horses?'

Gay: 'Sure, honey. Nevada mustang. Used to ship them

all over the United States once upon a time. Mostly gone now, though.' He turns back to Guido: 'We'll have to pick up another man.'

'Dayton Rodeo's on today. We could probably find a fella down there.'

'Hey, that's an idea! Roslyn, you never saw a rodeo.'

Isabelle: 'Oh, you gotta see a rodeo.'

Roslyn: 'I'd love to. If you come with us, Iz.'

'I'm all set.'

Roslyn springs up. 'I'll get dressed up!' She quickly looks at Gay. 'Let's have some fun today!'

Gay: 'Now that's a girl! Get goin' right now.' He gets up and shoos her toward the bedroom, and as she starts away he grabs her hand and she turns back to him, her face warmed by the return of his connexion with her. 'Honey, when you smile it's like the sun comin' up.'

He lets her go and she flies toward the bedroom.

Six

THE four are silent in the station wagon as they drive into the sun on the empty highway. Gay drives with one hand resting on Roslyn's bright silken dress where it flows off her thigh.

Behind them Guido blinks at time passing by. 'I'd like to have stopped home and got cleaned up a little.' He feels his stubble, glancing ahead at Roslyn's brushed hair.

She turns back to him. 'Why? You look nice, Guido. Doesn't he, Iz?'

'Better than a lot I've known.'

Guido smiles moodily. 'You're just one mass of compliments, Isabelle. Hey! Hold it!' He grabs Gay's shoulder, at the same time spinning around in his seat to look at something they have passed. 'Stop!'

Gay brakes the car, and Guido points back toward a bar and gas station. 'The guy next to that phone booth. I think it's that kid from California. Back up!'

Gay turns and cranes out the window. 'What kid?'

'That what's-his-name – the rodeo rider was working the Stinson Rodeo with you last year.'

'Perce Howland?' Gay shouts and backs the car along the highway, fast.

Perce Howland is sitting on his saddle, his back against a glass-enclosed phone booth beside the highway. He is resting his chin on his hands, his eyes staring at the bare ground. Noticing the reversing car, he looks toward it with sleepy eyes. He is in his late twenties, a bucking horse rider – which is to say a resident of nowhere, who sleeps most often in his clothes, rich and broke in the same afternoon, celebrated in the lobbies of small hotels where a month earlier he might have been thrown out for loitering. He does not yet have the cauliflower ear, the missing front teeth, or the dazed eye of his tribe, but his face has been sewn and his bones broken.

Glancing up at the approaching car on the deserted highway, his eyes already show their expectant, seeking quality. There is a naïveté in his strangely soft, gentle movements, a boyishness which is itself a force.

A great glad smile opens on his face as he sees through the side window of the car coming to a halt before him. He gets up and goes to the car. 'Gay Langland! Why, you old buzzard, you!'

Gay grabs his arm. 'What are you sittin' out here for?'

'I hitched a ride to the Dayton Rodeo but the fella changed his mind and left me here. Hey, Pilot, how you doin'? Boy, it's sure good to see you two scoundrels!'

Gay draws Roslyn closer to his window. 'Like you to meet this fella, Roslyn. This is Perce Howland.'

She nods.

Perce removes his hat. 'Well, old Gay is sure comin' up in the world. How do, ma'am.' He shakes her hand; there is a certain embarrassed shyness on him. He regards her as one of Gay's passing divorcees.

Guido starts to introduce him to Isabelle when the bell rings inside the phone booth. Hurrying toward it, he carefully puts his hat on as though he were to face someone in there.

' 'Scuse me, I been tryin' to call home but they keep puttin' me into Wyoming!'

He steps into the booth and closes the door. 'Hello, Ma? Perce, Ma.'

The four in the car sit in silence, listening to his muffled voice. Perce's emotion quickly reaches them, holding them still.

'Hello? You there? It's Perce, Ma. I'm okay. No, I'm in Nevada now. I *was* in Colorado. Won another bull-ridin', Ma. Hundred dollars. Yeah, real good rodeo. I was goin' to buy you a birthday present with it but I was comin' out of my boots. . . . No, Ma, I haven't been in a hospital since I told you. I just bought some boots, that's all, Ma.' Astounded: 'What in the world would I want to get married for? *I only bought some* –' He breaks off. 'Whyn't you try believin' me once in a while, make everybody feel better, huh?' She is obviously berating him. 'Okay, okay, I'm sorry.' Trying to bring brightness back: 'They give me a silver buckle on top of the prize money!' Holding the buckle of his belt toward the phone: 'Got a buckin' horse on it and my entire name wrote out underneath. Ain't you proud?' His smile goes; he touches his cheeks. 'No, no, my face is all healed up, good as new. You will too recognize me! Okay, operator! Ma? say hello to Frieda and Victoria, will ya?' A silence. He is being severely instructed and his patience is waning. He opens the door for air. Sweat is burning his eyes. 'Okay, say hello to him, too. No, Ma, it just slipped my mind, that's all. . . . *Okay*, I'm sayin' it now.' Near an outburst: 'Well, you married him, I didn't! Tell him hello for me. Maybe I'll call you Christmas. . . . Hello? Hello!' He is cut off, but with a deeply troubled mumble he adds: 'God bless you too.'

His sombre look is disappearing as he comes out on the sidewalk. He is a little embarrassed at having shown so much emotion before these others, and he tries to laugh, shaking his head and mopping his face. 'You wouldn't be goin' down to the Dayton Rodeo, would you?'

Guido: 'Why? You entered?'

Perce: 'I aim to if I can get a ride out there. . . . And if I can raise ten bucks for the entrance fee. . . . And if I can get a loan of a buckin' horse when I get down there.' He laughs. 'I'm real equipped!'

Gay: 'How'd you like to do some mustangin' with us? We need a third man.'

Perce: 'Boy, you still flyin' that five-dollar airplane?'

Guido: 'Lot safer than a buckin' horse.'

Perce: 'Lot higher, too, comin' down.'

Roslyn: 'Your plane that bad?'

Gay: 'Now don't start worryin' about him, honey.'

Roslyn, laughing: 'Well, I just asked.'

Gay, to Perce and Guido: ''Cause if she starts worrying, she can *worry*.'

Perce is surprised and drawn toward her intensity. 'You got a right to if you ever seen that D C-six-and-seven-eighths he flies. I didn't know they still had mustangs around here.'

Guido: 'I spotted fifteen this morning.'

Gay, quickly: 'Well, there might be more, though.'

Perce: 'What're you gonna get outa fifteen?' He laughs, not knowing why. 'Like if there was a thousand or somethin' it'd make some sense. But just to go up there and take fifteen horses . . . I mean the *idea* of it, y'know? Just kinda hits me sideways.'

His sensitivity seems to move over into Roslyn's face. She seems grateful he is there.

Gay: 'It's better than wages, ain't it?'

Perce: 'Hell, anything's better than wages.'

Gay: 'Tell you what. We'll drive you down to the rodeo, put up ten for the entrance fee, and I'll get a loan of some good stock for you down there. You come along with us tomorrow morning and help us run some mustang.'

Perce thinks for a moment, then says: 'And you buy a bottle of good whisky right in there so I'm primed up for the rodeo.'

Gay: 'Just wait right there.' He starts into the bar, putting his hand in his pocket.

Perce turns to Roslyn, intense curiosity and excitement in his face. He cannot place her. 'You an . . . old friend of Gay's?'

'Pretty old.'

He nods slightly, and awkwardly turns, as though escaping the insoluble, and goes to get his saddle to put it into the car.

Seven

THEY are driving through a new kind of territory. There is not even sage here, but only a sterile white alkali waste. It is midday.

Gay is at the wheel, Roslyn beside him, Guido and Perce in the rear seat. Guido has a whisky bottle tilted to his lips. They are all a little high. Guido passes the bottle to Roslyn over her shoulder; she silently drinks, then hands it over to Gay who takes a short one and hands it back. Guido never takes his brooding eyes from Roslyn. She makes a half-turn in her seat and gives the bottle to Perce, who drinks and then holds the bottle on his knee, staring out at the white waste going by.

Their eyes are narrowed against the harsh light. They have been driving a long time. Now Gay overtakes a horse-van trailer hitched to a new car, and as they pass it Perce leans out his window and waves at the Stetson-hatted cowboy driver. Then he speaks to Roslyn, resuming a conversation that had died out.

Perce: 'I've broke this arm twice in the same place. You don't do that fakin' a fall, y'know. I don't fake anything. Some of these riders'll drop off and lay there like they're stone dead. Just putting on a show, y'know. I don't fake it, do I, Gay?'

Gay: 'That's right. You're just a natural-born damn fool.'

Roslyn: 'Why! That's wonderful ... to be that way?' To Perce: 'I know what you mean. I used to dance in places ... and everybody said I was crazy. I mean I really tried, you know? Whereas people don't know the difference.'

Guido, who has been looking at her feverishly, as though his several concepts of her were constantly falling to pieces: 'What kind of dancing you do?'

Roslyn, with embarrassment: 'Oh . . . just what they call interpretive dancing. Night clubs. You know.'

Perce sticks his head in between her and Gay. 'I went to a night club once – in Kansas City. Name of it was "The Naked Truth". And they wasn't kiddin', either!'

He laughs, but an uneasiness on her face dampens him.

Gay calls out, 'Here we come!'

Their attention is drawn to the first glimpse of the town. A long, gradual curve of highway lies directly ahead, an arc of concrete raised above the valley bottom of white gypsum. At the distant end of the road is a row of wooden buildings and beyond them the mountains piled up like dumps of slag the colour of soot. From this distance the desolation is almost supernatural, the mind struggling with the question of why men would ever have settled here. There is no tree, no bush, no pool of water. To right and left the blank white flatland stretches away, dampened here and there by acid stains of moisture left from the spring rains. Gradually a perverse beauty grows out of the place. It is so absolute, its ugliness is so direct and blatant as to take on honesty and the force of something perfectly defined, itself without remorse or excuse, a town set up beside a railroad track for the purpose of loading gypsum board from the nearby plant.

Gay and Guido have been here many times for the yearly rodeo, Perce and Roslyn never. As the road straightens and they can see into the town's interior, the silence which has held them is broken by Gay explaining, with a grin, that this is the last wide-open town in the West. There is no police force and practically no law. Except for this one day there are never strangers here, and most of the natives are related closely enough to settle disputes among themselves. He is grinning but he is not making light of his instruction to her to stay close to him. There is no help here; there will not necessarily be trouble, but there has been, and they still carry sidearms in this place, and use them. 'Like in the movies,' Roslyn says, her eyes wide with incipient laughter, but they do not laugh – not entirely because of fear but from a sense of absurdity, the kind of absurdity so senseless as to rise to a logic, a law, a principle of destruction, as when one is knocked down by a bicycle and killed on the way to a wedding. Without warning, they realize that the town is packed with people, perhaps two thousand, a mob boiling around on the highway between the row of buildings and the railroad tracks. Its uproar strikes at them through the car windows, a clash and rumble of humanity enslaved by its own will a hundred miles out in this sun-stricken powderland.

Gay slows the car to avoid the first humans, men standing in the middle of the highway, talking, looking into the windows as they pass. Now there are cars parked along the roadside, jalopies mostly, and some recent models caked with talc. The door of one of them swings open; a girl of twelve runs out with a little boy, and they dash toward the dense mob as though they knew where they were going. An old man stands peeing in the sun and chewing a wad of tobacco as he turns with the car passing him by. Gay can barely move ahead now as the car is engorged by the crowd.

Perce suddenly sticks his head out the window. 'There's old Rube! Hey, Rube! Whatcha say!' Rube waves back. 'Hey, there's old Bernie! Whatcha say, Bernie!' Bernie waves back. Perce draws his head into the car and leans in between Gay and Roslyn. 'Hey, they got some real riders here today! Hope I draw me a good horse!'

Gay: 'Just come out in one piece, now, 'cause you gotta go mustangin' tomorrow.'

Roslyn is looking at Perce's face, a few inches from her eyes; she sees the pure lust for glory in him. A new emotion flows from her toward him – a kind of pity, a personal involvement in his coming trial.

He jerks away to call out the window again: 'There's Franklin! Hey, Franklin boy!'

The car moves into the heart of the crowd.

There are cowboys in working clothes, and many in the tight shirts and jeans they saw in movies. There are many kids, dressed like their elders. There are farmers in overalls, women in Sunday best. A cowboy is trying to back a horse out of a little trailer van right into the stream of traffic; three girls not yet sixteen walk in front of a gang of cowboys who are trying to make them; a mother holds on to her teenage daughter's wrist as she pushes through the crowd. Two overweight deputies, with .45s hanging from their hips, bounce a Cadillac up and down to unhook its bumper from a battered pickup truck behind it. In the pickup is a gang of kids with a farmer driving. In the Cadillac, its convertible top down, are three betting types and a show girl, all bouncing up and down and striving to retain their dignity and their sunglasses.

Above the people and the cars, mixed with their roar, is a cacophony of jazz; each bar's jukebox is pouring its music into the street, one number changing to another as the car passes the screen doorways. An enormously loud voice from a nearby public-address system announces something indistinguishable; then there is the sound of a crowd roaring as in a stadium – the rodeo arena is in action at the far end of the street.

Roslyn suddenly turns to watch an Indian standing perfectly still while the crowd pours around him. He is staring off at something – or at nothing – with a bundle of clothes under his arm.

Gay nudges his car to the left, even letting the fenders press people out of the way, and pulls up facing one of the bars. He takes Roslyn's hand and draws her out of the car past the steering wheel; the four, with their arms raised against the crush of people, squeeze into the saloon. The dog sits up in

66

the front seat, looking around calmly, seeing everything, turning her head from one familiar face to another. An old man comes out the screen door, sees the dog, and goes to the window to look in at her. She looks at him. He is bleary. His shirtfront is streaked with tobacco juice. Deep blackheads swarm around his nose. He reaches into his pocket and takes out coins from which powdery talc sifts down. He tosses a quarter to the dog and she sniffs it on the seat. and looks back at him in puzzlement. He winks at her and disappears into the crowd with his secret.

The sound of money clinking turns people around; a sweet little old lady is hurrying through the crowd, violently shaking a well-filled collection can. She wears a toque hat askew on her grey head and a brocade dress down to her shins. Something like 'Oyez, oyez,' is coming out of her voice box, and she is smiling wittily under incensed, climatic eyes. She pulls the screen door open and pushes into the saloon.

This bar is fifty feet long. The customers are ranked back to the opposite wall and order drinks from a distance the width of a handball court. There is a spidery atmosphere of a hundred hands raised to pass drinks back and empties returning to the bar. Two jukeboxes are playing different records and a television set on high is speaking, its eye rolling in its head. Five bartenders face the mob, serving and collecting, grimly glancing right and left along the mahogany to ward off any attack upon the vertical platoon of bottles behind them. Overhead, reflected in the yardage of the mirror on the wall, a morose elkhead stares through the smoke. A printed sign hanging from a piece of twine around its neck reads, 'Don't shoot this elk again', and the careful eye can see the bullet holes that drew sawdust instead of blood.

The old lady pushes up to a cowboy and his girl at the bar and shakes the can under their surprised faces.

Old lady: 'Church Ladies' Auxiliary, Tom.'

'Sure.' He drops a coin in the collection can.

67

The old lady turns to his girl. 'How about you, sinner?'

'Oh, Ma! I got no money yet!'

The old lady shakes the can at another prospect nearby. 'Come on, Frank. Church Ladies' Auxiliary.'

'You just got me in the bar next door.'

'That'll larn you to stay put. Come on!'

He groans and puts in money.

Roslyn, Gay, Perce, Isabelle, and Guido, with drinks in hand which they can barely raise to their lips, are pressed together at the bar, standing in the paralysing noise like people in a subway. A grizzled old man with startling silver hair forces his way through and hoists a seven-year-old boy on to the bar. Holding the boy's knees, he explains to Gay, 'I gotta hold on to him tight or first thing y'know he run off to school.'

Gay nods understandingly, and the old man smiles through his haze, 'Hya, Coz, not many of us left.'

'Well, things are tough all over, Pop.'

The old man yells at the bartender: 'Draft of pop for my grandson Lester!' He is full of holiday cheer and, taking a paddle-ball from the boy, he says to Gay: 'Ever try one of these? Damnedest thing I ever saw. Stand clear, now!'

With which he swats away at the elusive ball, while people around him shield their faces from his unpredictable blows. The bartenders come alert.

Roslyn has found room to get her glass to her lips and drinks fast, calling: 'Hey, I can do that! Can I try?'

The old man, sensing action, offers her the paddle at once. 'Betcha two dollars you can't do ten!'

Perce: 'I'll take that! Go ahead, Roz!'

Roslyn, untwisting the rubber band: 'Oh, I can do more then ten! I *think*!'

Pushing his back against the crowd, the old man spreads his arms. 'Clear away, clear away, we got a bet goin'!'

News of a bet miraculously squeezes the crowd back, and a space opens around Roslyn. She starts to hit the ball and does it obviously well. She has a drink still in one hand. Perce counts each stroke, two dollars in his hand. By the time she gets to six, a cowboy yells at Perce: 'Five bucks she don't do fifteen!'

Perce, nodding and still counting: 'Nine, ten, eleven . . .'

Perce reaches toward the surprised old man, who hands him the two dollars.

Second cowboy: 'Ten she don't make twenty!'

Perce: 'Thirteen, fourteen, fifteen, sixteen, seventeen, eighteen, nineteen, twenty, twenty-one, two, three, four, five, six . . .' Perce collects from both cowboys, counting on. From all over the saloon voices call new bets and money passes in all directions.

'Ten here too!'

'Five here!'

'I'll take five!'

'Fifteen here!'

Roslyn is now working the ball with great earnestness, sipping her drink at the same time, an alcoholic distance spreading in her eyes. Isabelle, counting aloud with Perce, picks up her drink and takes a gulp and looks at it with disgust. She sees a bottle of whisky and pours some into her glass, drinks, and sets it down. The little boy sitting on the bar beside her, his eyes fascinated at Roslyn's attack on the ball, lifts his pop glass – which Isabelle has just inadvertently spiked – drinks, and studies the new effect upon him, and tastes some more.

The crowd is roaring out Roslyn's count now. The little old lady, trying to push through the circle of men who have formed around Roslyn and Perce, manages to peep through the bodies, and her eyes fasten on the growing wad of money in Perce's upraised hand. With a new spurt of greedy determination she pushes through to Perce who calls: 'Thirty-six, thirty-seven, thirty-eight, thirty-nine, forty! Forty-one, forty two . . .'

Suddenly she starts hitting the ball at the floor and receiving it back on the bounce. A roar of excited appreciation goes up at this new risk she is taking. Even the bartenders are on tiptoe, stretching to see over the crowd.

'Ten bucks she don't do seventy!'

Perce nods, takes the money without losing his count: 'Fifty-four, fifty-five . . .'

A second cowboy suddenly steps out and pats Roslyn low on the back. Guido, standing beside Gay, looks and sees Gay's mild irritation. Gay now scans the faces in the crowd. The eyes around him are coursing Roslyn's body. Guido bursts out laughing: 'She'll do anything!' and Gay sees in Guido's expression the same near-lewdness of some of the crowd. A new shout goes up.

Now she is hitting the ball on the bounce, and backhand, taking a drink at the same time. Perce is continuing his count at her side, absorbed, young, somehow at one with Roslyn as he urges her on with his counting. The old lady steps up close to Roslyn, calling into her ear as she shakes the collection can. 'Play for the Lord! Steady, sinner!'

Roslyn, unnerved: 'Please!'

Old lady to Perce, demanding the money in his hand: 'Help the good work, boy, do it while the spirit's in ya.'

Perce: 'Seventy-one, seventy-two, *shut up*, four, *seventy-five* . . .'

A shout goes up at this new victory. Roslyn is now a foot from the second cowboy with her back to him, and he grabs her from behind and starts to kiss her. Gay is on him and is about to hit him when he is pulled away by others. Two bartenders leap the bar. Guido appears next to Gay and draws on his arm, grabbing Roslyn with his other hand; he pulls both of them toward the door.

The old man turns to his grandson on the bar, and is about to take the boy down when he notices the bemused look in his face. He takes the half-full glass out of his little hand, sniffs it, then tastes it. First surprise penetrates his fog, and then with a genuinely avaricious wheedling tone, 'Lester!' he asks, bending down into the boy's somnolent face, 'where'd you get the money?'

On the street outside, Gay draws Roslyn out of the mob into a space between two parked cars. Just behind them, Perce, Guido, and Isabelle are counting the money in Perce's hat. Moved by his protective passion, Roslyn clasps his face. 'I'm sorry, Gay, I didn't mean to do it that long! But thanks for helping me! I embarrass you?'

The threat of losing her in the moments earlier, the lust of others for her, has wiped out his reserve. 'I'd marry you.'

Roslyn, with a sad and joyous mixture: 'Oh, no, Gay, you don't have to! But thanks for saying that.'

Perce bursts in, Guido behind him. 'Hundred and forty-five dollars! Ain't she great, Gay? She is the greatest yet!'

With which Perce throws an arm around her as he puts the money in her hand. Instantly the old lady appears under Perce's arm, shaking the can.

Isabelle: 'Don't shake that at me! I'm still payin' off this broken arm!' Suddenly Isabelle, seeing someone in the crowd, shouts, 'Charles!' and runs into the passing mob.

The old lady, shaking the can under Roslyn's face, fixes her with her missionary stare. 'Sinner! I can tell you want to make a big donation. You got it in the middle of your pretty eyes. You're lookin' for the light, sinner, I know you and I love you for your life of pain and sin. Give it to the one that understands, the only one that loves you in your lonely desert!'

At first amused, then drawn and repelled, then half-frightened, and yet somehow reached by this woman's mad desire to bless her, she starts to hand the old lady the whole wad of money.

But Gay intercepts. 'She ain't sinned that much.' He

hands the old lady one bill. 'Here's ten . . .' He gives her another. 'And here's ten more to settle for the twenty.'

Old lady: 'Lord be praised! We're gonna buy a fence around the graveyard, keep these cowboys from pasturing their horses on the graves. Sweetheart, you've gone and helped our dead to rest in peace! Go reborn!'

Isabelle rushes up to Roslyn out of the crowd. 'Guess who's here! Dear girl, guess who is here!'

'Who?'

'My husband! I couldn't believe it. They're on vacation.'

'Oh. His wife too?'

'Sure! Clara. You remember my talkin' about Clara, she was my best friend? And she's sweeter than ever!'

Gay: 'Sure must be, to make you so glad to see her.'

'Oh, Charles could never've stayed married to me. I even lost the vacuum cleaner once.' The men burst out laughing, and she joins them, and waves her arm toward her former husband, who is evidently somewhere deep in the crowd. 'They still haven't found it! Come, you'll meet them.'

Gay stops them. 'Let's meet you later, Isabelle. We still got to get this boy a horse to ride.'

'Okay, we'll be around someplace. But I won't be mustangin' with you – they're gonna stay at my house for a week.' She reaches for Perce's hand and squeezes it. 'Good luck, young fella!' Patting Roslyn's hand, she backs into the moving crowd, waving happily. 'See you, dear girl!'

Pressed together by the surrounding crowd, the four move toward the end of the street and the rodeo arena. Perce puts his head between Gay and Roslyn. 'Can I kiss her for luck?'

'Once.'

Perce kisses her as they move.

Gay draws him away from her. 'You don't need all that luck. Come on, let's get you registered.' He starts off ahead with Perce, laughing over his shoulder to Roslyn. She waves to him as he vanishes into the crowd.

The rodeo arena is a home-made corral surrounded by a collapsing post-and-rail fence, with splintered bleachers three tiers high along one side. A chute of planks is at one end and near it a low tower for the judge. A sea of parked cars surrounds the area. From the stands the only visible building is a small church leaning in the direction of the distant mountains, its cross of boards twisting under the weight of weather into the form of an X.

The stands are packed and the mob has surrounded the fence. There is always a certain threading movement of people looking for one another – fathers for their daughters, wives for husbands, fellows for girls, and loners from the hills who want only to move through the only crowd of strangers they will touch until the same time next year.

A rider on a bucking horse charges out of the chute. The timing judge in the tower, his stop watch in his hand at the end of a heavy gold chain, drinks from a pint bottle, his eyes flicking from watch to rider. The contestant is staying on the black horse. It charges directly toward the fence and the crowd there clambers backward, and for a moment the Indian is left in the clear, watching impassively. The horse swerves away, the crowd surges back, and the Indian is lost among the people again.

Roslyn and Guido are in the stands. Guido looks on, half-interested. She is watching avidly. He turns and stares at her beside him, his eyes absorbing the moulding of her face, her neck, her body.

The crowd roars suddenly, and people around them half-stand in their seats. Alarm shows in her face as she stands. The rider scoots from the horse's flying hooves.

'Gee, I didn't know it was so dangerous!'

Guido, deliberatively, as though declaring his determination toward her: 'Same as everything else worth doing.'

She looks at him with surprise. Whisky and sun have dissolved his strategy, and he simply stares longingly into her

eyes. She turns to see the outrider coming alongside the bucking horse and undoing its bucking strap.

'What'd he just take off?'

'Oh, that's the bucking strap. Grabs them where they
don't like it. Makes them buck.'

'Well, that's not fair!'

He starts to laugh, but her intensity stops him. 'You
couldn't have a rodeo otherwise.'

'Well, then you shouldn't have a rodeo!'

The crowd suddenly roars and stands, and she and Guido
rise, but he is staring at her with deep puzzlement as she turns
toward the arena where the bucking horse has chased the rider
over the fence. A few yards away Gay and Perce sit straddling
the closed chute, their legs slung over the top. Now Gay looks
at the people in the stands.

'I hope you're sober.'

Perce, following Gay's eyes: 'Hell, I've won prizes where
I couldn't remember the name of the town.' He sees Roslyn in
the stands and waves. 'There she is!'

Gay waves to her now and she stands up, waving her furred
sweater. Guido raises his arm.

Perce, seeing her passionate encouragement, turns to Gay.
'I wouldn't try to move in on you, Gay – unless you wouldn't
mind.'

Gay nearly blushes. 'Boy – I'd mind.'

They both laugh at this unwitting avowal of their conflict
and Gay slaps Perce on the back with warmth as a horse is
led into the chute at their feet.

'Well, here I go!'

Perce descends from the fence on to the restive horse with
Gay lending a hand, and he looks up at Gay.

'My address is Black River –'

He is cut off by the public-address system.

Public-address system: 'On a bucking horse, Perce Howland out of Black River, Wyoming!'

'California, not Wyoming!' he yells over his shoulder.

A cowboy pulls the bucking belt tight. The horse kicks the chute planks.

Gay: 'You ready, boy?'

Perce: 'Go! Go!'

Gay: 'Open up!'

An attendant opens the gate; the horse charges out. The crowd roars. Perce is holding on. The horse bucks under him, high and wild.

In the stands Guido has come alive. 'Go it, boy!'

Roslyn is looking on, torn between hope of Perce's victory and terror; she holds her hands to her ears as she watches.

The timing judge drinks, his stop watch in his hand.

From the chute fence, Gay glances at Roslyn in the stands. She is watching with tears in her eyes. The horse leaps in close to where she is sitting, and for an instant she can see Perce's teeth bared with the tension of his fight as he is flung up and down, the sky over his head.

The horse is twisting Perce, wracking his body as it comes down on the packed earth. Now she shouts as though to rescue Perce, calling his name. She turns to Guido for help. He strikes the air with his fist, a look of near-rage on his face, a flow of animal joy that disconcerts her, and, more alone now than before with her terror, she turns back to the field.

A sudden roar goes up from the crowd, and Gay rises up on the fence with a look of what almost seems like joy on his face, but his rising movement is to help. Perce is being thrown. He lands on his face and lies still.

Gay jumps down from the fence and runs toward Perce. Guido is pushing his way down the bleacher rows to the field; Roslyn remains standing on her bench behind him, stretching to see over the crowd, staring and weeping, her face as blank as if she had been struck. Now she starts down the bleachers toward the field.

Gay reaches Perce and starts to lift him to his feet. Guido arrives and they half-carry Perce toward a gate in the fence, Guido clapping his hat on to his head.

Roslyn catches up with them as they emerge into an area of parked cars. An ambulance is standing in front of the church.

Roslyn: 'Where's the doctor?'

Perce: 'Where's my hat, Pa?'

Gay: 'You got it on, Perce.'

Perce suddenly pulls away and yells at Roslyn, who has grasped his arm.

Perce: 'Lemme go, Frieda!'

Gay comes up to him, holding out his hand to calm him, 'Take it easy, boy, she ain't your sister.' Perce is staring, perplexed, at Roslyn. She is cold with fright. But they move him along again. They arrive at the ambulance. An attendant is waiting, an affable grin on his face. 'Well now, you've been messin' around with the wrong end of a horse, haven't you?' He holds Perce's face, pressing his cheekbones in his hair-covered hands.

Roslyn: 'Let him sit down.'

She sits him on the edge of the ambulance floor. The attendant's movements do not quicken. She looks distrustfully at him.

Roslyn: 'Are you a doctor?'

Perce starts to rise. 'I don't want a doctor.'

Attendant: 'Hold it, boy. I'm no doctor. I'll just clean you up a little.' He presses Perce down, wipes his hands on his trousers, and reaches into the ambulance for something.

Roslyn, with a growing feeling of helplessness: 'Well, isn't there a doctor?'

The attendant reappears with a bottle of alcohol and a swab.

Gay: 'Not for sixty miles.'

Gay bends and looks closely at Perce's face as the attendant swabs it; then he straightens up. 'He ain't bad hurt.'

'How do you know? Let's take him!' She reaches down to lift Perce. 'Come with me, I'll take you in my car.'

Gay, forcefully, not too covertly taking her from Perce: 'Now don't start runnin' things, Roslyn.'

'He's your friend, isn't he? I don't understand anything!'

A loud yelp of pain from Perce turns her about; the attendant is pressing adhesive tape across the bridge of his nose. Perce delicately touches his nose as Gay bends down to him where he sits on the edge of the ambulance floor. 'You all right, ain't you, Perce?' Perce exhales a breath of pain, then feels his nose.

'Perce, you all right?'

Perce blinks, looks up at Gay, still dazed. 'Did I make the whistle?'

'Almost, boy. You done good, though.'

'That was a rank horse. Wasn't it?'

'Oh, that was a killer. You done good.'

Perce tries to stand, but falls forward on to his hands and knees. Roslyn quickly bends to lift him up.

Gay: 'Leave him alone, Roz, he'll get up.' He separates her from Perce, who remains for a moment on all fours, catching his breath.

In horror, in a sea of helpless non-understanding, she looks down at him. Now he raises himself with great difficulty to his feet. Guido hands him his hat, which has again fallen off. The public-address system erupts, incomprehensibly.

Perce: 'Oh! That me?'

Gay: 'Not yet. You still got a coupla minutes.'

Roslyn: 'What for?'

'He's got a bull to ride. Come on, Perce, walk yourself around a little bit.'

Gay, putting Perce's arm over his shoulder, walks down an aisle of parked cars with him. Perce is not sure-footed yet, but is getting steadier. They walk slowly, in the sea of steel.

Roslyn: 'Guido, he's not going in there again!'

Guido, with an uncertain celebration of life's facts: 'I guess he wants to ride that bull.'

'But . . .' Frustrated, she runs to Gay and Perce and moves with them.

'Just let him walk it off, Roz, come on now.' Gay presses her aside.

She has to squeeze in beside them, sometimes forced behind them by an obstructing fender. 'What are you doing it for, Perce? Here, why don't you take what we won in the bar.' Struggling with her purse to get money out, she tries to keep up with them. 'You helped me win it, Perce, come on, take it. Look, it's over a hundred dollars. You don't have to go back in there!' He halts. She presses up to him. He is staring at her. She feels encouraged now. She gently touches his cheek, smiling pleadingly.

Perce: 'I like ya to watch me now. I'm pretty good ridin' bulls.'

'But why're you doing it?'

'Why, I put in for it, Roslyn. I'm entered.'

The public-address system again erupts incomprehensibly.

Perce: 'Get me up there, Gay, I'm just warmin' up!'

They start for the arena. She hurries along with them. Guido is following, still smiling at her concern. He is progressively drunker.

Roslyn: 'Gay, please!'

But Perce and Gay continue moving toward the chutes.

Perce turns to her over his shoulder. 'I like ya to watch me, Roslyn! Don't you be scared, now!'

Roslyn turns to Guido, who is standing beside her, as though for help. Beneath his troubled look she sees he is blandly accepting the situation. Reasonably, he says, 'They don't mind getting busted up!' She turns quickly, scanning the world for help. No human being is in sight – only row after row of cars, mute, iron. The roar of the crowd mixes with the babble of the public-address system.

The bloody-eyed face of an immense white Brahma bull appears under Perce and Gay where they sit on the chute wall. Its handlers are respectfully hogging it into position. Now a handler loops the bucking belt around the bull's hind quarters, letting it hang loose for the moment. Perce is wide-eyed with fear and calculation. He is blinking hard to clear his head and softly working a wad of tobacco in his cheek. Gay turns to him from the bull, which is now directly under them. In Gay's eyes is a look of brutal pride in Perce. 'You okay, boy? You want it?'

Perce hesitates, looking down at the bull; he has the excitement of one already injured. Then: 'Hell, yes.' He leans out over the bull to straddle it.

'Perce!'

He looks up and Gay does. Gay smiles pridefully, almost tauntingly, toward Roslyn, who has climbed the bottom rung of the fence a few yards away and is calling: 'Gay, don't let him! Perce, here's your prize! Why . . .' She holds out the money toward him. Guido, no longer smiling, is beside her.

She is cut off by the public-address system: 'Now folks, who do you think is back with us? We still got some real men in the West! On a Brahma bull, again, out of Black Hills, Colorado, *Perce Howland*!' The crowd roars.

Roslyn is struck dumb by the inexorable march of it all. She looks down, calling defeatedly: 'Gay!'

Gay helps as Perce descends and straddles the bull. Mounted, he turns up to Roslyn. 'You watch me now, sport!'

A handler yanks the bucking belt up tight. The bull shoots its head up, the gate opens, and Perce goes charging out into the arena.

Standing so close to the chute, Roslyn can feel the earth shake as the bull pounds out across the arena, and once having felt the thunder of its weight she nearly goes blind, seeing only tattered impressions that filled her through her fear: the bull's corded neck, it's oddly deadened eyes fixed on some motionless vision of vengeance, the pounding on the earth that seems to call up resounding answers from deep below the ground. The beast humps into the air and shifts direction, coming down, and Perce's body twists and doubles over, straightening only to be wracked again, flung and compressed as though he were tied to the end of a whip. A grimace of teeth-clenching anguish spreads over his face, and when he comes down from a leap his head is thrown back against the darkening sky like that of a supplicant. The crowd is roaring, but she does not hear it; customers are fighting the air with their fists and tearing with bared teeth at a hundred imagined demons, dogs are barking, pop bottles smash, strangers are squeezing one another's arms, a portable radio in the stands is loudly advertising an airline's cuisine, and the sun itself is setting behind the blind mountains; she is in a void, a silence of incomprehension, glimpsing only the bull's steady, remorseless stare and Perce's head snapping back like a doll's, the manly determination of his mouth belied by the helpless desolation in his eyes.

Guido has stopped cheering. Out of his half-drunken lethargy a new inner attention has straightened him, and he turns to her as though to comfort her, but she runs into the crowd behind her. A coarse call, a roar, an 'Ohhh' from the crowd turns her around to the arena.

Perce is lying in the dirt, his shoulder twisted over half his face. The silence of the mountains spreads over the arena and the stands. The barebacked bull is lunging and blindly kicking near Perce's body, and the outrider is trying to manoeuvre it toward the chute, his expression drained of sport, his body pivoting his horse with every threatened feint of the white bull.

Gay is running across the bull's path. He doubles back and around the turning bull; the outrider's horse shields him for a moment and he drags Perce along the soft sand to the fence. Guido helps him lift Perce over it.

The crowd is standing, watching in silence. The grunted, growling breathing of the bull can be heard now. A cloud of grey dust hangs over the arena, but is already being carried away by the rising night breeze.

Eight

DARKNESS brightens the neon glare from the bars, and bluish vestigial light still glows along the mountain ridges. Cars are parked tightly against the bar fronts, one of which has been pushed in, stucco facing hanging agape. The crowd is thinner now and moving at promenade pace. The families are leaving in their cars and trucks. There are many small squads of cowboys moving in and out of the bars, with one girl to a squad. Unknowable conversations are going on in parked cars, between the freights, around unlit corners, between man and man and man and woman, some erupting in a shout and strange condemnations, or laughter and a re-entry into the bars.

Roslyn is cradling her head in her arm in the front seat of the car. Her face is tired from weeping and she is still breathing shakily in the aftermath of a sobbing spell.

Gay calls her name from the window opposite. He has a wryness in his look, knowing she is displeased with him. 'Come on, honey, we're gonna have some drinks.' The hurt in her face makes him open the door and he sits beside her.

Roslyn: 'Is he still unconscious?'

Gay: 'Probably, but it ain't noticeable.' He turns his head and she follows his gaze through the rear window.

Perce, his head enormously wrapped in white bandage, is heatedly arguing with the rodeo judge behind the car. Guido is standing between them, blinking sleepily.

'He's arguing with the judge about who won the bull ride. You still mad at me?'

Her resentment gives way to relief at seeing Perce alive. Now she turns to Gay. 'Why did you hit me?'

'I didn't hit you. You were gettin' in the way and I couldn't carry him, that's all.'

'Your face looked different.' She stares at him now, a question in her eyes. 'You looked like you . . . could've killed me. I . . . know that look.'

'Oh, come on, honey. I got a little mad 'cause you were gettin' me all tangled up. Let's have some drinks, come on now.'

Roslyn, glancing back at Perce: 'He still hasn't seen a doctor?' Gay turns his back to her impatiently. 'He might have a concussion! I don't understand anything; a person could be dying and everybody just stands around. Don't you care?'

Gay returns to the seat beside her. With anger in his voice: 'I just went in for that boy with a wild bull runnin' loose – what're you talkin' about? I'm damn lucky I'm sittin' here myself, don't you know that?'

'Yes. You did.' She suddenly takes his hand, kisses it, and holds it to her cheek. 'You did!' She kisses his face. 'You're a dear, good man. . . .'

Gay, holding her, wanting her to understand him: 'Roslyn, honey . . .'

'It's like you scream and there's nothing coming out of your mouth, and everybody's going around, "Hello, how are you, what a nice day," and it's all great – and you're dying!' She struggles to control herself and smiles. 'You really felt for him, didn't you?'

Gay shrugs. 'I just thought I could get him out. So I did, that's all.'

Roslyn, her face showing the striving to locate him and herself: 'But if he'd died . . . . you'd feel terrible, wouldn't you? I mean, for no reason like that?'

'Honey . . . . we all got to go sometime, reason or no reason. Dyin's as natural as livin'; man who's too afraid to die is too afraid to live, far as I've ever seen. So there's nothin' to do but forget it, that's all. Seems to me.'

Perce sticks his head into the car. The tape is still on his nose, the bandage like a turban on his head. He is slightly high from the shock. Guido sticks his head in on the other side of the car.

Perce: 'Hey, Roslyn! Did you see me?'

'Oh, you were wonderful, Perce! Get in and we'll take you back to –'

'Oh, no, we got to have some fun now!'

Gay: 'Sure, come on!'

Roslyn hesitates, then: 'Okay. How do you feel?'

'Like a bull kicked me.'

Guido opens the door for her. Gay gets out on Perce's side of the car. As she emerges from the car she quietly asks Guido: 'Is he really all right?'

'In two weeks he won't remember this – or you either. Why don't you give your sympathy where it's appreciated?'

Roslyn, pointedly but with a warm laugh: 'Where's that?'

She walks past him; he follows. They meet Gay and Perce in front of the saloon

Perce: 'In we go!'

Gay has her arm as her escort; Perce is on her other side, his open hand wavering over her back but not touching her: he is recognizing Gay's proprietary rights. Guido walks behind them. They enter the crowded saloon and take seats around a table.

There is feverish intensity in Perce's speech and in his eyes. As they sit, he calls over to the bartender: 'Hey, whisky! For eight people.'

He gets into his chair. He is strangely happy, as though he had accomplished something necessary, some duty that has given him certain rights. He laughs, and talks without diffidence to Roslyn now. 'Boy, I feel funny! That man give me some kind of injection? Whoo! I see the prettiest stars, Roslyn.' He reaches for her hand and holds it. Gay, whose arm is over the back of Roslyn's chair, grins uncomfortably. Roslyn pats Perce's hand and then removes her own. Perce does not notice this, and again takes her hand. 'I never seen stars before. You ever see stars, Gay? Damn bull had the whole milky way in that hoof!' Gay laughs. Guido smiles with a private satisfaction. Roslyn is torn between concern for his condition and a desire to celebrate her relief that he is alive. 'Say, was that you cryin' in the ambulance? Was that her, Gay?'

'Sure was.'

Perce rises from his chair, fervently shaking her hand: 'Well, I want to thank you, Roslyn.'

A waiter puts two glasses of whisky before each of them, and Perce raises his high.

Perce: 'Now! Here's to my buddy, old elderly Gay!'

Roslyn: 'Gay's not old!'

Perce: 'And here's to old, elderly Pilot. And his five-dollar elderly airplane.' They all have glasses raised. 'And my friend, Roslyn! We're all buddies, ain't we, Gay?'

Gay grins to dilute the growing seriousness of Perce's meaning. 'That's right.'

The jukebox explodes with 'Charley, My Boy'.

Perce: 'Then what're you gettin' mad at me for, buddy? Can I dance with her?'

Gay: 'Sure! Roslyn, whyn't you dance with Perce?'

Roslyn: 'Okay.' She gets up and goes on to the dance area with Perce.

Guido: 'Nothin' like being young, is there, Gay?'

'That's right. But you know what they say – there's some keeps gettin' younger all the time.' He grins at Guido, who turns back to watch the dancers with a faintly sceptical smile. Perce is doing a flat-footed hicky step, and she is trying to fall into it with him. Half-kidding, he nevertheless seems to be

85

caught by an old memory, as he moves with straight-backed dignity.

'My father used to dance like this.' Now he twirls her around, and himself starts to circle her; a dizziness comes over him.

'What's the matter!'

'Whoo!'

She catches him as he stumbles. 'C'mon, let's see the world.' Taking her hand, he goes out a door in the rear of the saloon. She glances back to see Gay turning drunkenly in his chair, and she waves to him as she is pulled out through the back door.

They emerge behind the saloon. Trash, a mound of empty liquor bottles and beer cans, broken cartons, are littered about, but a few yards off the desert stretches away in the moonlight. He looks up at the sky and then turns to her. Wordless, he starts to sit on the ground, taking her hand and drawing her down, too, and they sit side by side on the sprung seat of an abandoned, wheelless car. Now he smiles weakly at her.

'Nobody ever cried for me. Not for a long time, any-way . . .' Full of wordless speech, longing to make love to her and be loved by her, he takes her hand. 'Gay's a great fella, ain't he?'

'Yes.'

'I want to lie down. Okay?'

'Sure.'

He lies in her lap, and suddenly covers his eyes. 'Damn that bull!'

She smoothes his forehead. Now he opens his eyes. 'Just rest. You don't have to talk.'

'I can't place you, floatin' around like this. You belong to Gay?'

'I don't know where I belong.'

'Boy, that's me, too. How come you got so much trust in your eyes?'

'Do I?'

'Like you were just born.'

'Oh, no!'

'I don't like to see the way they grind women up out here. Although a lot of them don't mind, do they?'

'Some do.'

'Did you really cry for me before?'

'Well, you were hurt and I –' She breaks off, seeing the wondrous shake of his head. 'Didn't anybody ever cry for you?'

'No stranger. Last April the twelfth, I got kicked so bad I was out all day and all night. I had a girl with me and two good buddies. I haven't seen her or them since.'

'They left you alone?'

'Listen . . . let me ask you something . . . I can't talk to anybody, you know?' She waits for him to speak. 'I . . . . I don't understand how you're supposed to do.'

'What do you mean?'

'Well, see, I never floated around till this last year. I ain't like Gay and Pilot, I got a good home. I did have, anyway. And one day my old man . . . we were out back and suddenly, *bam*. Down he went. Some damn fool hunters.'

'They killed him?'

'Uh-huh. And . . . she changed.'

'Who?'

'My mother. She was always so dignified . . . walked next to him like a saint. And pretty soon this man started comin' around, and she . . . she changed. Three months they were married. Well, okay, but I told her, I says, "Mama, you better get a paper from Mr Brackett because I'm the oldest and Papa wanted me to have the ranch." And sure enough, the wedding night he turns around and offers me wages. On my own father's place.'

'What does *she* say?'

Shaking his head in an unrelieved agony, and with a mystical reaching in his tone: 'I don't know; she don't *hear* me. She's all *changed around*. You know what I mean? It's like she don't remember me any more.'

She nods, staring.

'What the hell you depend on? Do you know?'

'I don't know. Maybe...' She is facing the distant horizon, staring at her life. 'Maybe all there really is is what happens next, just the next thing, and you're not supposed to remember anybody's promises.'

'You could count on mine, Roslyn. I think I love you.'

'You don't even know me.'

'I don't care.'

He raises his face to hers, but his eyes are suddenly pain-wracked, and he grips his head. 'That damn bull!'

The back door suddenly swings open, throwing the light of the saloon on them. Gay comes out, walking unsteadily, blinking in the sudden darkness. He calls: 'Roslyn?'

'Here we are!' She gets up with Perce.

Gay comes over, shepherding them toward the door. 'Come on, now, I want you to meet my kids.'

'Your kids here?'

'They come for the rodeo. I ain't seen them in a year. You oughta see the welcome they give me, Roslyn! Nearly knocked me over.' They go through the door and up a short corridor. 'She's gonna be nineteen! She got so pretty! Just happen to be here for the rodeo, the both of them! That great?'

'Oh, I'm so glad for you, Gay!' They go into the saloon.

Gay, now drawing Roslyn by the hand, and she holding on to Perce's hand, come up to the crowded bar, where Guido is standing in a drunken swirl of his own. The air is muddy with smoke and jazz. Perce is blinking hard, trying to see. Roslyn watches him even as she attends to Gay.

Gay reaches Guido first. 'Where are they?'

'Where are who?' Guido turns to him slowly.

'My kids! I told them I'd be back in a minute. You heard me tell them.'

'Went out there.' Guido points toward the door to the street, then looks appraisingly at Roslyn and Perce.

Gay looks hurt and angered, then pushes through the door and goes out. He looks about at the parked cars and the moving groups of people and the armed deputies, and he yells: 'Gaylord! Gaylord?'

Now Roslyn comes out of the bar, helping Perce. Guido is with them, carrying a bottle. Their attention is instantly on Gay, except for Perce, who immediately lays his cheek on the car fender, embracing it.

'Rose-May! Gaylord! Gaylorrrrd?'

Guido comes up beside Gay, a muddled, advice-giving look on his face. Roslyn remains holding on to Perce.

Guido bays: 'Gaylord! Here's your father!' He sways, pointing at Gay.

People are beginning to congest around them, some seriously curious, some giggling, some drunk. Roslyn remains with Perce just behind Gay and Guido, watching Gay, tears threatening her eyes.

'Gaylord, where you gone to? I told you I was comin' right back. You come here now!'

A woman, middle-aged, dressed like a farmer's wife, comes up to Gay. 'Don't you worry, Mister, you'll probably find them home.'

Gay looks at her, at the security emanating from her sympathetic smile. He turns and climbs up on to the hood of the car; he is very drunk, and shaken. He looks over the crowded street from this new elevation. Just below him Roslyn and Guido are looking up into his face, and he seems twice his normal size. Drunks mill around below, the bar lights blink crazily behind him, the armed deputies look on blankly from the doorways, and the jazz cacophony is flying around his ears like lightning. His hat askew, his eyes perplexed, and his

89

need blazing on his face, he roars out: 'Gaylord! *I know you hear me!*'

There is now a large crowd around the car, the faces of alien strangers. Gay bangs his fist on the roof of the car. 'I know you hear me! Rose-May – you come out now!' He suddenly slips on the hood and rolls off on to the ground, flat on his back. Roslyn screams and runs to him, as the crowd roars with laughter; she quickly lifts up his head and kisses him.

'I'm sure they're looking for you, Gay. They must've thought you'd left.' He stares dumbly at her. 'Oh, poor Gay, poor Gay!' She hugs his head and rocks him, crouched beside him in the gutter.

Nine

THE car is speeding on the dark highway. Guido is driving, the dog asleep beside him. In the back seat Roslyn has one arm around the unconscious Perce, whose legs hang out a window, the other arm around Gay, asleep against her breast. Her eyes are closed.

Suddenly the car bumps up and down, and Guido is trying to bring it back on the highway. For an instant the headlights catch a figure scurrying off the road shoulder. The car swerves back on to the highway. Now a man rises from the roadside, brushes himself off, picks up his bundle, and walks impassively on. It is the Indian.

The ride is smooth again, and Roslyn has opened her eyes. She is drunk and exhausted, a feeling of powerlessness is on her. Guido has a vague look of joy on his face as he drives. She speaks in a helpless monotone, as in a dream: 'Aren't you going too fast? Please, huh?'

'Don't worry, kid, I never kill anybody I know.'

The speedometer is climbing toward eighty.

'A fellow smashed up my best girl friend. All they found were her gloves. Please, Guido. She was beautiful, with black hair. . . .'

'Say hello to me, Roslyn.'

'Hello, Guido. Please, huh?'

His eyes are glazed and oddly relaxed, as though he were happy in some corner of his mind. 'We're all blind bombardiers, Roslyn – we kill people we never even saw. I bombed nine cities. I sure must've broken a lot of dishes but I never saw them. Think of all the puppy dogs must've gone up, and mail carriers, eyeglasses . . . . Boy! Y'know, droppin' a bomb is like tellin' a lie – makes everything so quiet afterwards. Pretty soon you don't hear anything, don't see anything. Not even your wife. The difference is that I *see* you. You're the first one I ever really *saw*.'

'Please, Guido, don't kill us. . . .'

'How do you get to know somebody, kid? I can't make a landing. And I can't get up to God, either. Help me. I never said help me in my life. I don't *know* anybody. Will you give me a little time? Say yes. At least say hello Guido.'

She can hear the murderous beating of wind against the car.

'Yes. Hello, Guido.'

From over ninety the speedometer begins to descend.

'Hello, Roslyn.'

Headlights hit the dark, unfinished house, illuminating the unfinished outside wall and the lumber and building materials lying around on the ground. Now the motor is shut off, but the lights remain on.

No one is moving inside the car. Guido, exhausted, stares at his house. The dog is asleep beside him. Now he opens the door and lumbers out of the car. He opens the rear door and blearily looks in.

Roslyn is sleeping, sitting upright. Perce is still asleep on her lap, his feet out the window; Gay is on the floor. Guido stares at her, full of longing and sorrow for himself. He looks down at Perce, then at Gay, and as though they were unbearably interfering he steps back from the car and walks into the darkness.

Loud hammer blows open Roslyn's eyes; Gay sits up. 'Okay, I'll drive, I'll drive.'

'We're here, Gay.'

'Where?'

She sees something in the headlights through the wind-shield; carefully she slides from under Perce's head and out the door, and walks unsteadily from the car toward the house, mystified. She walks in the headlight beams; the hammer blows are a few feet away. Awe shows on her face.

Guido is drunkenly hammering a sheathing board to the unfinished wall of the house. It is on crooked, but he gives it a final pat of satisfaction, then goes to the lumber pile and takes off another board, nearly falling with that, and lays it up against the wall, trying to butt it up against the previously nailed board. He hammers, as in a dream, the kind of pleasure and pain that comes of being freed of earthly logic, yet being driven toward some always receding centre.

Roslyn comes up to him, not daring to touch him. 'Oh, I'm sorry, Guido. Guido? I'm so sorry.' He continues dumbly hammering. 'Won't you hit your hand, it's so dark? It's dark, Guido, look how dark it is.' He hammers on. She almost turns, spreading her arms and looking skyward. 'Look, it's all dark!' A sob breaks from her. 'Please? Please stop!'

From nearby Gay calls angrily: 'What the hell you stompin' the flowers for?'

Roslyn turns to Gay, who comes up to Guido and swings him around by the shoulder and bends to the ground. 'You busted all the damn heliotropes!'

Gay is on his hands and knees now, trying to stand up the fallen flowers. Guido is looking down dumbly, the hammer in his hand.

Gay: 'Look at that! Look at that, now!' He holds up a torn stem. 'What in hell good is that, now?'

Roslyn: 'He was trying to fix the house.'

Rising unsteadily to his feet, Gay asks menacingly: 'What call *he* got to fix the house?'

Roslyn: 'Don't! Don't! Please, Gay! He . . . he's just trying to say hello. It's no crime to say hello.'

From behind them they hear Perce crying out: 'Who's doin' that?'

They turn to see Perce staggering into the headlight beams, trying to free his head and arms from yards of unravelling bandage flowing off his head. He is fighting it off like a clinging spider web, turning around and around to find its source.

'Who's doin' that?'

Roslyn hurries toward him. 'Don't! Don't take it off!' She reaches him and tries to unwind his arms.

'Get it off. What's on me?'

'Stop tangling it. It's your bandage.'

He stops struggling and looks at the bandage as though for first time. 'What for a bandage?'

Roslyn is starting to laugh despite her concern. A few yards away, Guido is quietly but deeply laughing, glassy-eyed. Gay is beginning to feel the laughter's infectiousness. Feeling a hysteria of laughter coming on, Roslyn tries to wind the bandage on again. 'It's for your head.'

Perce: 'My –' He breaks off as he raises his hands and feels the bandage wrapped around his head. 'I have this on all night?' He looks angrily at Guido and Gay, who are roaring now, and to them he says: 'Who tied this on me?' He is trying to pull it off his head.

She tries to stop his hands. 'The ambulance did it. Don't take it off.'

Perce, unwinding and unwinding the bandage: 'You leave me at a disadvantage all night? Who put it on? Gay, you . . .' He lunges toward Gay and trips on a board, and the whole pile of lumber topples on him with a great crash. Guido and Gay fall about, dying with hysteria.

Roslyn, between laughter and tears, tries to extricate Perce from the lumber. 'Get him up. Gay, come here. Guido! Carry him, please. He can't help himself.' The men come to help her, and still laughing crazily they lift Perce and almost carry him to the door of the house. She goes inside ahead of them.

Looped in their arms, Perce demands: 'Who put it on? Leave me at a disadvantage all night?' She and Guido get him through the door of the house. 'Where's this? Let me alone. Where is this place?' He lies on a couch as Guido sprawls on his favourite chair, catching his breath.

Roslyn: 'This is my house . . . or Guido's.' She laughs. 'Well, it's a house, anyway.'

Perce closes his eyes. Suddenly the house is quiet. She covers Perce with an Indian blanket, and the touch stirs him to resistance. 'No, Ma, don't, don't!' He turns his face away.

Now she stands and sees Gay sitting outside the door on the step. She goes down to him, starting to wipe the hair out of his eyes, and he takes her hand. A curious inwardness, a naked supplication has come into his face.

'Wish you'd met Gaylord, Rose-May. If I had a new kid now, I'd know just how to be with him, just how to do. I wasted these kids. I didn't know nothin'.'

'Oh, no, I'm sure they love you, Gay. Go to sleep now.'

He grasps her hand, preventing her from leaving. 'Would you ever want a kid? With me?'

She pats his hand, starting to turn away. 'Let me just turn the lights off in the car.'

He raises up, struggling to get on his feet.

'Whyn't you sleep now . . .'

'I don't wanna sleep now!' He staggers to his feet, swaying before her. 'I asked you a question! Did I ask you to turn the lights off in the car? What are you runnin' away from all the time?' With a wide gesture toward windows and walls that nearly tumbles him: 'I never washed the windows for my wife even. Paint a fireplace! Plant all them damn heliotropes!'

He suddenly goes to the doorway and yells into the house: 'What're they all doin' here? What're you bringin' them around for?'

'I didn't bring them, they just –'

'Where are you at? I don't know where you're at.'

Trying not to offend him and still speak her truth, she embraces him. 'I'm here, Gay. I'm with you. But . . . what if some day you turn around and suddenly you don't like me any more? Like before, when Perce got hurt, you started to give me a look. . . . . I know that look and it scares me, Gay. 'Cause I couldn't ever stay with a stranger.'

'Honey, I got a little mad. That don't mean I didn't like you. Didn't your papa ever spank you, and then take you up and give you a big kiss?' She is silent. 'He did, didn't he?'

'He was never there long enough. And strangers spank for keeps.' She suddenly presses herself against him and he embraces her. 'Oh, love me, Gay! Love me!'

He raises her face and kisses her. She smiles brightly.

Roslyn: 'Now we made up, okay?'

Gay: 'Yes, okay, okay!' Laughing softly, he hugs her.

'You sleep now . . . you're tired. Sleep darling.'

'And tomorrow I'll show you what I can do. You'll see what living is.'

She nods in agreement, gently pressing him to the doorway. He goes into the dark house, talking. 'We'd make out. I could farm. Or run cattle, maybe. I'm damn good man, Roslyn – best man you'll ever see. Show you tomorrow when we hit those mountains. Ain't many around can keep up with old Gay. You wait and see.'

She hears the bed groaning, then silence. She walks unsteadily to the car, reaches in, and pushes the switch. The lights go off. Now she stands erect and looks up at the oblivious moon, a vast sadness stretching her body, a being lost, a woman whose life has forbidden her to forsake her loneliness. She cries out, but softly, to the sky: 'Help!'

For a long time she stands there, given to the dreadful clouds crossing the stars, racing to nowhere.

Ten

A PLUME of dust is moving across the desert, following Gay's old but still serviceable truck. On the open bed, lashed to the back of the cab, is a drum of gasoline with a hand-cranking pump protruding from its top. It is bumping along over the sage, here and there crunching a whitened skeleton of winter-killed cattle.

Gay is driving; Roslyn beside him has the dog in her lap, its muzzle on her shoulder. Perce spits out the window. His nose is still taped. The sun narrows their eyes. They bump along, facing the desert before them.

Roslyn can feel the dog shivering. She looks at it, then turns to Gay. 'Why is the dog shivering?'

'She'll do that up here.'

Suddenly Guido's plane zooms down over the roof of the cab and they see it flying straight ahead of them a few feet off the ground toward the mountains, its wings waggling a greeting. They shout in surprise. Gay waves out the window and speeds up the truck. His face and Perce's gain excitement, the knitting together of action.

True night is covering the mountains; it is the end of twilight, when the purple light is turning blue. Splashes of stars are tumbling on to the sky. The mountains, secretive and massive, wait. At their foot, the campfire shimmers – the only moving thing in the world.

The four are sitting around the fire. Nearby stands the

truck, and a little farther away the lashed plane, both flickered by moon and firelight like intruding monsters resting before an onslaught.

A hiatus in the talk. Guido is telling a story, unable to keep his eyes from Roslyn across the fire from him. She is putting away the last of the dried dishes into the tote box. Now she listens raptly. Gay is idly going through the dog's fur for fleas, and Perce waits for Guido's next word, full of respect for him.

Guido looks skyward. 'That star is so far away that by the time its light hits the earth, it might not even be up there any more.' He looks at Roslyn. 'In other words, we can only see what something was, never what it is now.'

Roslyn: 'You sure know a lot, don't you, Pilot?' Perce shakes his head.

Guido: 'Oh, astronomy's all in the library books. Nothin' to it but reading.'

Roslyn looks up at the sky. 'Still, it's wonderful to know things.'

'You got something a lot more important.'

'What?'

Guido, glancing up at the sky: 'That big connexion. You're really hooked in; whatever happens to anybody, it happens to you. That's a blessing.'

Roslyn, laughing: 'People say I'm just nervous.'

'If there hadn't been some nervous people in the world, we'd still be eating each other.'

Gay, suddenly clapping his hands as though to clean them: 'Well, I don't know about you educated people, but us ignorant folks got to hit the sack.'

He gets up; a certain tension between him and Guido has sharpened his movements.

Roslyn: 'Why is the dog shivering?'

Gay looks at the dog, then glances toward the mountains. 'Got a whiff of those horses, I guess. They must be close by, Guido.'

98

Roslyn has stretched over to stroke the dog. Suddenly it bares its teeth and nearly snaps her hand. She leaps away, terrified.

Gay is instantly furious. 'Hey, you damn fool! Come here!' The dog crawls to him on her belly and he slaps her.

Roslyn: 'Oh, don't hit her, she didn't mean anything! The horses ever kick her or something?'

Guido: 'It's not the horses she's afraid of.' They all look at him. He has the compact look of one who is taking a stand. 'It's us.'

Gay: 'What're you talkin' about now, Guido? I never mistreated this dog.' His anger is sharpening now.

Guido, holding his position, pitched high: 'Just common sense, Gay. She's been up here enough times to know what's going to happen. There's wild animals up there that'll be dead tomorrow night.'

There is a flare of astonishment in Roslyn's face. But the men all assume she knows this and Guido goes right on. 'How's she know she's not next? They're not as stupid as people, you know.'

Gay unrolls Roslyn's bedroll beside the fire. 'Here now, honey, you can keep yourself nice and warm by the fire.'

Guido has busied himself with his bedroll. Perce, however, is caught by the look in her face.

And now Gay, looking up from her bedroll, finds that she has not moved, and a strange look of fright is on her face.

At last she turns to him. 'You kill them?'

'No, no, we sell them to the dealer.'

Roslyn, her voice small, incredulous, even as somewhere in her this news does not come as a surprise: 'He kills them?'

Gay, with complete neutrality, as a fact: 'They're what they call chicken-feed horses – turn them into dog food. You know – what you buy in the store for the dog or the cat?'

She has begun to quiver. He goes to her and starts to take her hand kindly. 'I thought you knew that. Everybody . . .'

She gently removes her hand from his, staring incomprehensibly into his face, turns, and walks into the darkness.

'. . . knows that.' He hesitates for a moment, then, as much to cover his embarrassment before Guido and Perce as anything else, he picks up her bedroll and starts after her. 'Maybe you better sleep on the truck. In case something comes crawling around. . . .' He walks after her into the darkness.

He comes on her beside the truck, tosses the bedroll aboard, and smooths it out. She is staring wide-eyed, shaking slightly. He turns her to him. Slowly she raises her eyes to him. In her face we see the astonishment and the agony she feels as two contrasting ideas of him clash in her mind.

Gay: 'Get some sleep now. Come on.'

He starts to lift her aboard, but she gently stops him – gently enough to tell him how afraid of him she is. She is looking at him as though she had never seen him before.

'Honey, I just round them up. I sell them to the dealer. Always have.'

But her stare is unbroken.

'No need to look at me that way, honey. Now you're looking at *me* like a stranger.'

The imminent threat of her estrangement breaks his heart and he sweeps her into his arms with a muffled cry: 'Honey!'

He holds her away so he can see her.

Roslyn: 'I . . . I thought . . .'

'What?'

'They were for riding, or . . .'

'Sure, they used to be – especially Christmas presents for kids. 'Cause they're small horses, you see, the kids loved them for Christmas. But' – he almost smiles – 'kids ride motorscooters now. Used to breed them a lot too; mustang puts a lot of stamina into a breed.'

She is beginning to listen, to perceive a dilemma in which he too is caught.

'When I started, they used a lot of them I caught. There

was mustang blood pullin' all the ploughs in the West; they couldn't have settled here without somebody caught mustangs for them. It . . . it just got changed around, see? I'm doin' the same thing I ever did. It's just that they . . . they changed it around. There was no such thing as a can of dog food in those days. It . . . it was a good thing to do, honey, it was a man's work, and I know how to do it. And I wanted you to see what I can do.' He smiles. 'Aside from sittin' around the house and movin' furniture.'

'But they kill them now.'

He is silent, struggling for an answer.

'You . . . you know it's not right, don't you? You're just saying this, but you know.'

Gay's own guilt has been touched, and he cannot carry it alone. 'Honey, if I didn't do it, somebody would. They're up here hunting all the time.'

'I don't care about others!'

'You ate that steak tonight, didn't you? And you –'

Roslyn claps her hands to her ears. 'I don't care!'

'You've bought food for my dog, haven't you? What'd you think was in those cans?'

'I don't want to hear it!'

'Honey, nothin' can live unless something dies.'

'Stop it!'

She clambers aboard the truck, climbs into the bedroll, turns on her side, and covers her eyes with her hands. He hesitates, then hoists on to the truck bed and sits next to her. He knows he has all but lost her; only her evident agony tells him that parting will not be easy for her. At last, talking to her hidden face: 'Roslyn, we never kidded, you and I. I'm tellin' you I don't want to lose you. You got to help me a little bit, though. Because I can't put on that this is all as bad as you make it. All I know is – everything else is wages; up here I'm my own man. And that's why you liked me, isn't it?'

A silence grows.

'I liked you because you were kind.'

'I haven't changed.'

'Yes. You have. This changes it.'

'Honey, a kind man can kill.'

'No he can't!'

'Well, if it's bad, maybe you gotta take a little bad with the good or you'll go on the rest of your life runnin'.'

She suddenly faces him, her eyes full of tears. 'What's there to stop for? You're the same as everybody!'

She bursts into disappointed weeping, covering her face. In a moment he lays a hand on her. 'Yes. Maybe we're all the same. Including you.' She uncovers her face, starting to raise on her elbows indignantly. His voice is calm again. 'We start out doin' something, meaning no harm, something that's naturally in us to do. And somewhere down the line it gets changed around into something bad. Like dancin' in a night club. You started out just wanting to dance, didn't you? And little by little it turns out that people ain't interested in how good you dance, they're gawkin' at you with something altogether different in their minds. And they turn it sour, don't they?' Memory dissolves her anger, and she lies back. 'I could've looked down my nose at you, too – just a kid showin' herself off in night clubs for so much a night. But I took my hat off to you. Because I know the difference.'

Her eyes search his. He looks off at the dark mountains.

'This ... this is how I dance, Roslyn. And if they made somethin' else out of it, well ... I can't run the world any more than you could. I hunt these horses to keep myself free. That's all.'

Roslyn: 'You ... take your hat off ... to me?' He bends and kisses her on the lips. 'You mean it, don't you! Oh, Gay!'

They hold each other in the silence. He comes down off the truck bed. With troubled eyes he leans down and holds his mouth on hers and she presses his shoulders down upon her.

He stands erect, touches her eyelids. He goes from her to

the diminishing fire, sits on his bedroll, and takes off his shoes. Perce and Guido are in their bedrolls nearby. The dog comes and lies down, and Gay mutters: 'Shame on you, you fool.' He climbs into his bedroll.

Guido turns in his bedroll. 'I could fly her back in the morning, if you want me to.'

Gay simply looks at Guido with an instinctive, as yet unformed, suspicion.

Guido: 'I was wondering how she agreed to come up here.'

Perce flicks a cigarette into the fire. 'She's got a lot of right. If you come to think of it, it don't make too much sense for fifteen horses.'

Gay sighs. 'Don't worry yourselves about her now. She's comin' along fine.'

He turns on his side. Beside him the dog lies with head on paws, the firelight flickering on its eyes. Its breathing is still short and rapid. Gay, to the dog, very softly: 'You quiet down now. Everybody's showin' off.'

No one moves. Beyond the circle of light the land is empty. The night is filled with the firelit eyes of the dog, which blink toward the mountains and the still unseen animals that are to die.

Eleven

THE first rays of dawn are brightening the sky. Perce is on
the truck bed, cranking gas from the drum into the plane.
Guido is on top of the wing, holding the hose and peering into
the tank.

Gay walks over to a mound partially covered with drift
sand. He reaches down, grasps something, and pulls; a
tarpaulin is peeled off, revealing a dozen truck tyres. On the
wing Guido raises his hand, peering into the tank, and calls:
'Okay, hold it!'

Gay calls to them from the pile of tyres: 'Let's go, Perce,
gimme a hand here!'

Perce hops off the truck, gets in behind the wheel, and
backs to the tyres. Guido clambers down off the wing, reaches
into the open-sided cockpit, and draws out a shotgun pistol,
which he proceeds to load from a box of shells.

Roslyn, who is rolling up the bedrolls and tying them,
happens to look and sees the pistol in Guido's hand, hesitates,
then returns to her job. The dog comes up to her. She smiles
down at the animal, then with some initial fear reaches down
and pats it. Happily she calls: 'She's not snapping any more,
Gay!'

Gay is just heaving a truck tyre on to the bed of the truck
with Perce's help. He turns to her, smiling. 'Things generally
look a little different in the morning.'

Guido calls from the plane: 'I guess I'm ready, Gay!'

He is drawing out of the plane a shredded Air Force jacket

whose lamb's-wool lining is visible through slits in the outside leather. He and Gay go to each wingtip and unlash the plane. Perce goes to the tail and unlashes it. Roslyn comes near and watches now. Perce now comes alongside her and stands. Gay walks back to the cockpit with Guido.

Gay: 'How you want her?'

Guido looks up at the sky, holding a palm up to feel the breeze. He points: 'That way.'

Gay goes to the tail, lifts it, and swings the plane to face the direction of take-off. Then he walks along the plane to the propeller and waits. Guido is about to get into the cockpit.

Roslyn, as though to relieve the weirdly charged atmosphere, calls rather gaily to Guido: 'Boy, that's some jacket! Little breezy, isn't it?'

Guido: 'Went on a lot of missions in this thing. Wouldn't take a hundred dollars for it . . . bullet proof.' They chuckle as he climbs in and sits. To Roslyn: 'Glad you decided to stay with us. Probably never see this again in history, y'know.'

Roslyn: 'Take care, now.'

Guido mutely thanks her for her solicitude. 'Okay, boy, turn your partner and doe-see-doe! Switch off!'

Gay glances behind him to see if there is any obstruction to his back step, reaches up, turns the propeller several times. Guido slips his goggles on.

Guido: 'Switch on! With feeling now!' They laugh. Gay turns the propeller until it is horizontal and pulls down hard, but the engine does not start. 'And again! And let us pray.' Gay with special care grasps the propeller, pulls down. The engine huffs and dies. 'That's that damn car gas for ya. Okay, let's try her again.'

Again Gay yanks down on the propeller. The engine smokes, huffs, and with a sudden resolution clatters up to a roar. Guido straps himself in, lays the pistol in his lap, and with a wave to them guns the engine. The plane moves away from them, gains speed, and takes the air. Now it wheels in air and comes back, roaring over their heads and away toward the mountains. They turn with it.

The three squint against the prop blast. Gay is the first to move; he looks for an instant at Perce and Roslyn. They feel his glance. Without reason, they feel separated from him, and he smiles.

Gay: 'Here we go.' He turns toward the truck and starts to walk, Perce and Roslyn following him.

Guido lifts his goggles and looks up at the clear blue sky. His lips move as though in prayer. He lowers his goggles and looks down. The barrier face of the mountains suddenly passes under the plane. Now the sharp interior walls and steep valleys show, manless, half in shadow, with patches of grass here and there. A hidden secret world is opened. The plane flies just within the crests of the mountains, turning with the valleys, which Guido scans through the open-sided cockpit. Suddenly his head moves sharply.

Instantly he pulls the stick back; the plane abruptly climbs. Now he banks and turns, the plane shuddering on uneven steps of air. Now he checks his instruments and grasps the pistol in his right hand. With a glance over the side to aim himself, he presses the stick forward and dives.

The herd is coming up to him fast. Now the animals start to gallop along the wall of the valley. Guido flattens his dive and zooms in over the horses, his wingtips only yards from the valley walls. He pulls the stick back and the plane noses upward; he points the pistol down as he passes over the herd, and fires. With the shot the horses surge ahead even faster. He is conscious of having held his breath, of having felt a strange tremor in his engine at the moment of acceleration. With a sigh he flies toward the sky, turns tightly, lines himself up with the herd, and once more starts his dive.

The truck bumps along on the sage desert, but now it crosses a border where the sage and soil end and a prehistoric lake bed begins. It is a floor of clay, entirely bare, white, and flat as a table. Now the truck halts close to a little hummock bordering the lake bed.

Perce emerges as the engine is turned off. He looks around as Roslyn comes down out of the cab. Gay comes from the other side of the truck and walks around to them where they stand scanning the lake bed. The silence is absolute. There is no wind.

Roslyn: 'It's . . . like a dream!'

Set between mountain ranges the lake bed stretches about twenty-five miles wide and as long as the eye can see. Not a blade of grass or stone mars its absolutely flat surface, from which heat waves rise. In the distance it glistens like ice.

Perce: 'I seen a picture of the moon once. Looked just like this.'

Gay: 'He'll be drivin' the horses out of that pass.'

She and Perce look toward an opening in the mountain face perhaps a mile away. 'Does anybody own this land?'

'Government, probably. Just call it God's country. Perce? Let's get that drum off.'

Gay goes to the truck, hops on to the bed, and proceeds to unlash the gasoline drum. Perce stands on the ground and helps jimmy the drum to the edge of the truck. Now Gay hops down and both men let it down to the ground and roll it off to one side. Roslyn watches for a moment, then goes to the cab and leans in. The dog is quivering on the floor of the cab. She reaches toward it tentatively.

Gay goes to one of the tyres; he draws a rope from inside it and experimentally circles it over his head and throws it.

Perce, seeing him occupied, walks over to the cab and looks in from the side opposite to that of Roslyn. She is pressing her face against the dog's. Then she reaches up to the rear-view mirror, turns it to look at herself, sees Perce, and smiles.

He speaks as though voicing a premonition: 'I'd be a little careful what I said to Gay. For a while out here.'

Gay's face appears beside his. 'Got to get the glasses.'

Perce steps aside. Gay moves into the truck doorway, hardly looking at Roslyn, who now shakes dust out of her hair in the rear-view mirror. He reaches behind the seat and draws out a large binocular case. Looking at her now, grinning, an uncertainty still in his eyes, he takes the binoculars out of the case and puts the glasses to his eyes. Perce is watching him. He holds the glasses up to his eyes for a long moment, looking toward the pass.

She steps over to Gay, forcing a bright tone: 'See anything?'

Gay, putting the glasses on a tyre on the truck bed: 'Climb up, make yourself comfortable. He'll be a while yet.'

He gives her a boost. She mounts the truck bed. He climbs up and sits inside a pile of two tyres, his legs hanging over the edge at the knees, his armpits supporting his trunk.

Gay: 'Go ahead. It's comfortable.'

She does as he did; Perce mounts on to the truck.

Roslyn: 'It is comfortable! Try it, Perce.'

Perce does the same. The three sit in silence as Gay again raises the glasses and looks through them.

Gay turns to her. 'You lookin' real good today, honey. Maybe tonight we go down to Reno and dance, okay?'

'Okay.'

'I'd of brought your umbrella for you but I didn't think of it.'

'I'm all right. It's not too hot.'

She reaches over and touches his knee reassuringly, for she sees his anxiety about her. Now she withdraws her hand, and scans the lake bed.

Gay, for a moment, continues looking at her profile. He has sensed the dampened quality of her feeling. He turns and

108

glances at Perce, who is on his other side. Perce is staring toward the pass, clearly preoccupied.

For a moment Gay sits staring straight ahead; then he turns to her. 'I forgot to tell you something last night.'

She looks at him with quick interest.

'Lots of cow outfits use the pastures up in those mountains, and when they find mustangs there they just shoot 'em and leave 'em for the buzzards. 'Cause they eat up all the good grass, see.'

She nods that she understands, but he sees he has not pierced her dampened air, and he turns to Perce.

'You know that, don't you, Perce?'

'Huh? Oh sure, I know that.'

'Whyn't you say so?'

'I just said so.'

Gay raises the glasses. 'Nothin' but misfit horses, that's all they are, honey.'

He studies the pass through the glasses. Putting the glasses down, he turns to her with a warm memory in his eyes. 'Wished you'd been here in the old days.' Stretching an arm, toward the pass: 'They'd come pourin' out of those passes three, four, five hundred at a time. And we'd build us a big corral out here and funnel them right in. Some of them were real beautiful animals, too. Made sweet riding horses.'

For a moment she feels the breadth of his memories. 'It must have been wonderful.'

'Best life any man could've had.'

'I wished I'd been here . . . then.'

Perce: 'I hear something.'

Gay: 'What?'

Perce: 'Tick, tick, tick, tick, tick.'

Gay: 'It's my watch.'

Roslyn: 'Boy, it's quiet here! You can hear your skin against your clothes.' She tries to laugh.

Gay, exhaling, relaxing in the tyre: 'Ayah!' He leans back, closing his eyes. Perce and Roslyn, in effect, are becoming joined by a viewpoint toward Gay, who at every moment seems to be gathered up by a quickening forward rhythm. They look at each other, forced, as it were, to an awareness of looking on him with the same eyes.

Perce: 'I hear something!'

Gay listens. He raises the glasses, sees nothing, puts them down.

Gay: 'What?'

Perce: 'Engine, sounds like.'

They listen.

Gay: 'Where?'

Perce, indicating with an open hand the general direction of the pass: 'Out that way.'

Gay, after listening for a moment: 'Too soon. He wouldn't be in the pass yet.'

Roslyn: 'Wait.' She listens. 'I hear it.'

Gay strains to hear. Now a certain pique is noticeable in him because he can't hear it. 'No – just your blood pumpin' in your head, is all.'

Roslyn: 'Ssh.'

Gay watches her. Perce is also tensed to listen.

Gay: 'I always had the best ears of anybody, so don't tell me you – '

Perce, suddenly pointing, and screwing up out of the tyre to sit on its rim: 'Isn't that him?'

The three look into the distant sky, Roslyn and Gay trying to locate the plane, at the same time wriggling out of the tyres, to sit on the rims.

She suddenly cries out and points. 'I see it! There! Look, Gay!'

Almost insulted, he scans the sky, then unwillingly raises the glasses and sees the mountain pass up close; flying out of it is the plane, tiny even in the glasses. He puts down the glasses, blinks his eyes hard. 'He never worked this fast before. I'd've seen him but I didn't expect him so soon.'

Perce: 'I could see him glinting in the sun. It was the glint. That's why.'

Gay seems to accept the apology. Now, very distantly, an explosion is heard.

Roslyn: 'What's that?'

Gay: 'He fired a shot.'

She watches the pass with growing apprehension and fascination. Perce glances at her in concern, then back to the pass. They are all perspiring now in the warming sun.

Gay: 'I've sat here waitin' two-three hours before he come out. That's why I didn't see him.' Now, however, he glances at Perce and nods. 'You got good eyes, though, boy.' He raises the glasses again. Silence. They watch the pass. The sun is higher; heat waves rise around them like a transparent sea. Suddenly Gay straightens.

'There they come. One ... two ... three ... four ... five ... six. I guess he'll go back for the others now.'

Perce: 'Give me a look, heh?'

Gay hands Perce the binoculars. 'See the others yet?'

'No. There's ... six. And a little colt.'

Roslyn's flesh moves; she shifts the position of one hand to relax her tension.

Gay notices her shock without facing her, and he asks Perce: 'You sure?'

'Ya. It's a spring foal.'

Gay, watching the pass, can feel Roslyn's deepening stillness beside him.

Perce keeps the glasses up. 'It's a colt, all right.' He lowers the glasses and faces Gay. He speaks with finality, not quite accusing, but nevertheless with an implication of question as to what will be done with it: 'It's a colt, Gay.'

Gay, concerned, but with barely a look at Perce, takes the glasses. Perce turns to watch the pass again. Roslyn is staring at Gay's profile as though it were constantly changing in her mind. Now Gay lowers the glasses, faces her fully. He will not be condemned. 'Want a look?'

He gives her the glasses. She hesitates, but then raises them to her eyes. The lenses find the herd, galloping in file, the colt bringing up the rear with its nose nearly touching its mare's tail. Now the plane dives down on them and they lift their heads and gallop faster. The image shakes, as her hands lose their steadiness, then flows out crazily as the strength goes out of her hands. She sits there, blind.

Gay stands, and raises the glasses again. She wipes her fingers over her eyes. Another shot is heard. She opens her eyes to look. Perce and Gay are fixed on the distant spectacle. She gets to her feet and hops down off the truck. Perce looks to her.

She is barely audible: 'Maybe it's cooler in the truck.' She walks to the cab and climbs in.

Gay and Perce remain on the truck bed, sitting on the tyres again. Gay, with a glance, notes Perce's new uneasiness.

'It's all right. She's goin' to make it fine.'

Perce makes no attempt to reply. A challenge has somehow grown up before him. Their posture and movements relax now.

Perce: 'I thought you said there was fifteen. There's only six.'

'Probably lost a few. That'll happen.'

'Don't make much sense for six, does it?'

'Six is six. Better'n wages, ain't it?' Perce doesn't answer. 'I said it's better than wages, ain't it?'

Perce, with damaged conviction, looking at his shoe soles: 'I guess anything's better'n wages.'

They sit in silence. Then Gay crosses his legs.

'Perce? We've just about cleaned 'em out up here, but if you're interested in some real money, there's a place about a hundred miles north-east – Thighbone Mountain. I never bothered up there 'cause it's awful tough to get 'em out. You gotta horseback up in there. But I believe there must be five hundred on Thighbone. Maybe more.' Perce is silent, staring at the pass. 'There'd be *real* money. You could buy yourself some good stock, maybe even a little van – hit those rodeos in style.'

Perce cannot look at him. His voice oddly quiet, he says: 'I don't know, Gay. Tell you the truth, I don't even know about rodeos any more.'

'I'm beginnin' to smell wages all over you, boy.'

'I sure wish my old man hadn't of died. You never saw a prettier ranch.'

'Fella, when you get through wishin', all there is is doin' a man's work. And there ain't much of that left in this country.'

They are brought bolt upright by a ferocious snarling of the dog and Roslyn's screaming. Both of them leap off the truck bed as Roslyn jumps out of the cab, going backward. Gay rushes to the cab and sees the dog on the seat, its teeth bared, snarling.

Roslyn: 'She was shaking so I –'

Gay reaches in and throws the dog out of the truck. With tail between its legs, it crawls back to him. He reaches in behind the seat, takes out a length of cord, ties it to the dog's collar, and lashes the dog to the bumper. The dog crawls under the truck in the shade and lies down. Gay now goes to Roslyn, who is quivering; he starts to put his arm around her.

Roslyn halts and looks up into his face as though he must do something to calm the animal immediately. 'She's scared to death, Gay!'

'Well, even a dog can't have it just right *all* the time.'

The ring of his voice meets the sharp sound of a shot close by. It turns him toward the sky, and he immediately starts toward the truck, walking sideways as he talks to her behind him. Perce, a few paces away, turns to look for the plane.

Gay: 'Just roll with it, honey, and see how you make out just this once.'

He gets to the truck and immediately reaches behind the seat and draws out two iron spikes and a short-handled sledge-hammer. Now he glances for an instant toward the plane, which is just completing a dive. It is much closer now, its wing dents visible. The horses are galloping straight toward the bare white lake bed, but they are still on the sage-dotted desert.

All business now, Gay walks past Perce, who is staring at Roslyn. She is looking toward the horses. 'Give us a hand here, Perce.'

Perce, his eyes grown dreamy and strangely inward, follows Gay, who hands him a spike. He props it up as Gay drives it into the ground, ties a rope to it, and then, after pacing off several yards, does the same with the second spike and ties a rope to that.

Now Gay leaves Perce, walks to the truck, and tosses the hammer in behind the cab. For an instant he glances at Roslyn. She is wide-eyed, staring off at the horses. Gay passes her again, unties the dog, leads it to one of the spikes, and ties it there. The three stand in silence, watching the plane and the horses, which have reached the border of the white lake bed and have broken file, scattering right and left in order to remain on the familiar sage desert, frightened of crossing over into the strange, superheated air coming off the clay. Two of them have turned back toward the mountains and a flare of hope brightens Roslyn's face.

The plane lays over on one wing in a long climb and dives down, down on the horses within a yard of their heads. Guido has turned them, and now they break out on to the lake bed, re-forming their herded grouping. The plane now flies above the lake bed itself and is not climbing for another dive.

Gay takes Roslyn's arm and walks her quickly to the truck cab, but she resists entering. They stop.

'Up you go, honey.'

Before she can speak he hoists her into the cab, slams the door, quickly puts his head in, turns her face to him, and kisses her lips. 'Now you watch some real ropin'!' With great joy he steps away and leaps up on to the truck bed. Perce is still on the ground, indecisively standing there. 'Git up there, Perce, let's see what you can do now!'

Perce feels the force of Gay's command, and also sees what is evidently Gay's victory – for Roslyn is sitting motionless in the cab. He leaps aboard the truck bed.

The plane is just touching down on the lake bed and taxiing toward the truck. The horses are now trotting only, but so far away they seem like specks of illusion.

As the plane comes in fast, Gay hands Perce the end of a webbing strap whose other end is buckled to the post at Gay's corner. Perce passes the strap across his back and buckles the end to the post at his corner, so that both men are held, if rather precariously, to the cab and cannot fall backward. Gay now turns to the pile of tyres behind him and takes out a coil of rope from the top tyre. This Perce does too, from the pile behind him. Both men heft their ropes, grasping them a foot behind the nooses, turning them until the twist is out of them and they hang limber.

The plane taxis up, and the motor stops as it comes between the two spikes driven into the ground. Guido jumps out of the cockpit and runs to one spike, then the other, lashing the ropes to the plane struts. The dog, leashed to one of the spikes, snarls at him but he brushes it off and ties the rope. With his goggles on his forehead, his face puffed with pre-occupation, he trots over to the cab and jumps in behind the wheel. Without a glance at Roslyn he turns the key, starts the engine, puts the truck in gear, and roars off at top speed across the lake bed, peering ahead through the windshield.

'Grab hold now, we're gonna do a lot of fast turning.'

She grasps the dashboard, excitement pumping into her

face. The faded Air Force insignia on his shoulder is next to her face.

Through the windshield the open lake bed spreads before them. A mile off, two black dots are rapidly enlarging. Now their forms become clear: two horses standing, watching the oncoming truck, their ears stiffly raised in curiosity.

She turns to Guido. His goggles are still on his forehead; a look of zealous calculation is coming into his face. She is feeling the first heat of real terror, and turns to look forward, her hands grasping the dashboard tighter. The two horses, a hundred yards off now, their rib cages expanding and contracting, their nostrils spread, turn and gallop, keeping close together. Guido steers right up to the flying rear hooves of the horses. Now they wheel, and Guido turns sharply with them – the truck leaning dangerously – and works brake and gas pedal simultaneously. Now the horses run straight, and in doing so they separate from each other by a foot or two; Guido presses the truck into this space, which quickly widens, and he speeds even faster. Now there is one horse on each side of the truck, running abreast of the cab windows.

Roslyn looks at the horse running only a yard to one side of her. She could reach out and touch its eyes. It is a medium-size brown stallion, glistening with sweat. She hears the high screaming wheeze of its breathing, and the strangely gentle tacking of its unshod hooves on the hard lake bed. It is stretching out now, and its stricken eyes seem blind and agonized. Suddenly, from behind, a noose falls over its ears and hangs there askew.

On the truck bed, Perce is whipping his rope to make its noose fall over the stallion's ears.

Guido, unable to see him, yells to him past Rosyln's face, and he is calling with such urgency that he seems furious. 'Go on, get him! Throw again, Perce!'

At this instant Roslyn sees the other horse beyond Guido's

head as a noose falls cleanly down over its neck. Guido calls out the window on his side: 'Attaboy, Gay!'

Up behind the cab, Gay and Perce squint against the wind tearing at their hatbrims and their shirts. Gay, having just lass'd his horse, is now letting go of the rope, his horse swerving off to the left, away from the truck. The rope stretches to its limit, then suddenly yanks the heavy truck tyre off the top of the pile behind him. The horse feels the pull of the dragging tyre and the suffocating squeeze of the noose, rears in air, and comes to a halt.

The truck has never slowed. Perce, who has coiled up his rope, circles it over his head and throws it. The noose falls over the stallion's head. Veering away to the right, it pulls a tyre off from behind Perce.

Gay shouts with joy: 'That's the way!'

Perce returns a grateful look and Gay stretches and claps him on the shoulder, laughing. They are suddenly joined.

Guido steers sharply to reverse the truck's direction; Roslyn is looking out the window at the stallion being forced to a halt by the dragging tyre. Now it turns with lowered head to face the tyre; now it raises up in the air, its forefeet flailing. Suddenly the truck speeds up again, changing direction.

Roslyn turns to Guido and yells: 'Won't they choke?'

Guido: 'We're comin' back in a minute.'

They are speeding toward three rapidly enlarging specks; forms emerge; the three horses turn and run. Now a fourth, that of the colt, appears from behind the screening body of the mare. The colt runs with its nose in the mare's long, full tail.

Both men are twirling their lassos over their heads, leaning outward over the truck's sides. The sound of clattering hooves grows louder and louder in their ears. Gay's body absorbs the motion of the truck, his hands gently guide the rope, giving it form and life, and a startling pleasure shines in his eyes.

Perce is now above and a length behind the big mare and her colt. He is readying his noose, getting set. Suddenly Roslyn's head sticks out of the window of the cab, looking up at him pleadingly. She is almost within arm's length of the colt, which is galloping beside her. The fright and pain in her face surprise him. And Gay yells against the wind: 'Get that horse!' Now Gay throws his noose at the horse on his side, and Perce throws his rope. It lands over the mare's head and she veers to the right, the colt changing course with her. He turns and watches the mare being halted by the dragging tyre, the colt running almost rib to rib with her.

The one remaining horse is trotting away toward the brushy edge of the lake bed and the safety of the nearby hills. Guido sees it and speeds across the distance, and Gay lass's this horse a few yards before the sage border; once it is caught Guido circles back, leaving it bucking and flinging its heavily maned neck against the remorseless noose. Straight ahead in the far distance all of them see the stallion. While the other horses stand still, some of them with drooping heads, the stallion is flailing at the rope with his forefeet, charging toward the tyre and snapping at it with his teeth.

Guido speeds toward him, glancing at Roslyn. 'Now we tie them up so they don't choke. We'll pick them up to-morrow morning in the dealer's van.'

She is staring at the approaching stallion, and when he has stopped the truck beside it he merely gets out with a rope in his hand without turning back to her.

Gay and Perce have hopped off and Guido joins them. They are thirty feet from the animal, sizing him up. His sweat has blackened him, and he shines in the sun. Gay and Guido move toward him, spreading out. Their steps are quiet and all their movements small. The horse, seeing men for the first time, suddenly stamps down on the clay and, twisting his head, flies to one side. He is yanked off balance by the tyre rope, and stumbles on to his shoulder and springs up again. His wind is

118

screeching in his throttle now and blood is trickling from one nostril, and he is lowering his head to cough. The men advance, hefting their ropes.

Roslyn: 'The others are his mares?'

Perce, who is still near the truck, turns quickly and sees Roslyn looking at him from the window. He nods. 'That was his colt.'

Gay: 'Get on that tyre, Perce!'

The command sends Perce running away to the tyre, which is sliding behind the stallion; in air now, the animal comes down awkwardly on his hind feet and runs a length, and Perce jumps on to the tyre, digging his heels into the clay and holding on to the rope.

The stallion faces them again, groaning for air. The men stand still. Now Gay twirls his noose over his head and the stallion makes an abortive charge at Perce, who scampers off the tyre. As the stallion's profile for an instant presents itself to Gay, he flings his noose on to the ground; its right forefoot comes down as it runs past, and Gay jerks his rope and the fetlock is caught. Gay runs around the rear of the horse, flipping the rope over its back; on the other side he pulls in fast, and the right knee bends and the hoof is tight up against the stallion's ribs. Guido quickly throws and his noose sails over its face and behind its ears; with Perce holding the tyre rope taut from the neck, Guido half knee-bends with his rope over his thighs and pulls, and the two nooses squeeze now from opposite directions. They are choking the stallion down. On the other side of the animal Gay wraps his rope around his arm and with all his power leans back. The stallion's trussed right hoof is drawing up tighter and tighter into its ribs, and slowly it leans down until its knee hits the ground. Without for an instant releasing the tautness of his rope, Gay comes toward the stallion, hand over hand on the nylon, and when he is two feet away – Guido and Perce are still leaning with all their weight on their throttle nooses – he raises up one boot and, setting his heel on the stallion's shoulder, pushes so that the stallion rolls on to its right side. But as it falls its right hoof flies out, and the rope is yanked through Gay's glove. The men scatter as the stallion bursts up from the ground, running at them, springing high and twisting its body like a great fish springing out of water. Perce runs to the sliding tyre and digs in; the animal is jerked about by the neck and stands there, hawking air.

For a moment they are still. Now Guido walks softly and picks up his rope and Gay gets his, which is still noosed to the fetlock. After a moment when nothing moves but the horse's expanding and contracting rib cage, Gay suddenly flips his rope into the air over the horse's back, running around its rear at the same time, and once again he pulls and bends up the right leg. Faster this time, he comes in hand over hand to the stallion while Guido and Perce choke him down, and when he is close he jerks his rope suddenly and the horse goes down on to one knee. Now, to their surprise, its nose slowly lowers and rests on the ground as though it were doing an abeisance, blood running out of its nostrils on to the clay, its wind blowing up little puffs of talc. Gay pushes it over with his boot, and before it hits the ground he flips his rope around the left front fetlock. He knots both forefeet together and cuts the excess rope, stands away from the free hind feet, then delicately approaches, and with one movement wraps them together and draws them to the forefeet.

They have not heard her talking; Roslyn has come out of the truck and she is talking quietly. Only now in the quiet Perce senses her there and turns. She is smiling and her eyes are larger than life. 'Why are you killing them? Gay?' She begins to move toward the three men when a drumming in the ground turns them. The stallion has broken out of the truss and his hind feet are flailing free, his head beating the ground. Gay rushes to the tyre and pulls his head flat against the earth. 'Grab this, Perce!'

Perce takes the rope from him. Now he runs to Guido and grabs his rope, and circling behind the horse he twirls the noose over his head. The hind hooves are cracking against the forehooves and Gay knows the rope around the forefeet may tear. He throws and nooses both hind hooves together, comes around toward the head, and is drawing the hind legs up tight when he sees her hands.

She is pulling his rope, trying to get it away from him, and she is strangely smiling, calling into his face: 'Okay, you won – you won, Gay!'

'Get away, that horse is wild!'

'Oh, Gay, darling – Gay!'

Gay yanks his rope and swings his arm at the same time – for she is coming at him with her smile, and her fists are hitting his arm – and she goes flying backward and falls.

Perce is in front of Gay. 'Hey!'

For an instant they face each other.

Gay: 'Get on that tyre.'

'No need to hit her.'

'Get on that tyre, Perce. Don't say anything to me. Just get on that tyre and hold this horse!'

On the lake bed's silence they hear her sobs. They see her, all three turning now as she walks toward the truck, weeping into her hands.

Perce goes to the tyre and holds the neck rope taut. Gay trusses the stallion tight, four hooves together. Now Perce stands. None of them looks toward the truck. Gay lights a cigarette. They wipe the sweat off their faces. Her sobs come to them softly through the air. The three men and the stallion on the ground suck air. The horse coughs. Guido looks down at it, noting the old scars on its shoulders and quarters. One ear is bitten off at the tip. 'Boy, this son of a bitch must've kicked the shit out of every stud in Nevada.'

Perce sees now that Roslyn's muffled weeping has entered Gay, who stares down at the trussed stallion. 'I guess comin' up here the first time like her, there might not seem much sense to it at that, for only six horses. Not knowin' how it used to be.' An ironic, nearly bitter flicker of a grin passes over Gay's lips. 'I never thought of it, but I guess the fewer you kill the worse it looks.'

He raises his eyes toward the distance, and the two other men know his vision, the picture in his mind of the hundreds that once poured out of these passes. Gay glances down at the stallion once more. An embarrassment, almost a shyness, has crept over him as he turns to them. Even his stance seems suddenly awkward and not quite his own.

'What you say we give her this herd?'

Guido laughs; he does not believe it. But Perce reaches thankfully to grasp Gay's arm, when he sees Roslyn coming up behind them.

Gay faces her and his offer is dying in his throat at the sight of her eyes, the unbelievable distance in them, a coldness that seems to reach into her soul.

Roslyn: 'How much do you want for them? I'll pay you.'

The tendons stiffen in Gay's neck. With his eyes narrowed, he seems like a man being drenched.

'I'll give you two hundred dollars. Is that enough?'

'Let's get on the truck.' Gay is walking past her.

Perce almost leaps after him. 'But Gay! You were just sayin' you'd give them to her.'

Gay slows to a halt and thinks. The hurt is in his eyes like burning smoke. 'I did think of that. But I sell to dealers only. All they're lookin' to buy is the horse.'

Without moving toward him, her indignation still in her voice, Roslyn states as a fact: 'I didn't mean to insult you, Gay.'

'No insult. I was just wondering who you think you been talkin' to since we met, that's all.'

He walks to the truck and hops aboard. In silence the others take their places, Guido behind the wheel with her beside him, and Perce on the back with Gay.

Guido starts the engine and drives slowly toward the next horse they must tie up. He feels the waves of anger emanating from her. The silence between them gnaws at him. 'Brother, what a day.'

She does not speak or look at him.

'I nearly hit the side of that mountain before. Cylinder cut out just at the bottom of a dive. That's the closest I ever come, I tell you.'

She does not move. For a moment he can only glance at her in alarm, for she is evidently close to a state of shock.

'I . . . I know how you feel. I really do. . . .'

She is beginning to rock from side to side. Her alarm seems to require him to speak. 'Took me a while to get used to it myself. Tell you the truth, the only part of it I ever liked is the flying. Truthfully . . . you don't know me. I used to be afraid of too many things. I had to force myself. Because you can't run away from life, and life is cruel sometimes. . . .'

She claps her hands to her ears, a groan coming through her clenched teeth. It frightens him.

'Maybe you ought to wait in the plane. You want to? Look, I know how you feel but I can't stop it now. I know him. There'd be hell to pay!'

She looks at him directly, with a challenging contempt.

He suddenly senses a path for himself, a realization shows on his face, an excitement of a new kind.

'Listen, you want me to stop this?'

Her eyes open wide in surprise.

'You're through with Gay now, right?' She seems perplexed and he presses on against his own faltering. 'Well, tell me. He doesn't know what you're all about, Roslyn, he'll never know. Come back with me; give me a week, two weeks. I'll teach you things you never knew. Let me show you what

I am. You don't know me. What do you say? Give me a reason and I'll stop it. There'll be hell to pay, but you give me a reason and I'll do it!'

A power of contemptuous indignation has been rising in her, but he has seen nothing but what seemed to be her excitement at his offer. And when her voice strikes at him now, he almost leaps in surprise.

'A *reason*! You! Sensitive fella? So full of feelings? So sad about your wife, and crying to me about the bombs you dropped and the people you killed. *You* have to get something to be human? You were never sad for anybody in your life, Guido! You only know the sad words! You could blow up the whole world, and all you'd ever feel is sorry for *yourself*!'

A scream has entered her voice and it chills him. He stops the truck near the mare and colt and gets out. Guido seems transfixed as he walks around the truck to join Gay and Perce, who are hopping off the back. He moves up close to Gay, looks at the mare, and says in a peculiarly intimate, comradely way: 'Let's get the old lady, come on.'

'She's fifteen if she's a day.' Gay uncoils his rope, hefting it loose. The mare stands with her head stretched toward them, getting their scent. 'Probably wouldn't last the winter.'

Perce sees Roslyn turning away from the sight of the mare with a crazed look in her eyes. As Gay and Guido move toward the animal, the colt makes a bleating cry and runs a few yards and tumbles, rolling over and over, then springs up and runs back and collides with the mare, which does not budge.

Gay calls back over his shoulder, 'Perce!'

Perce walks slowly to the tyre and sits on it, grasping the rope.

The mare circles to keep Guido and Gay in front of her. They are easier in their movements with her than with the stallion; she moves more weightily because she is heavier and her foal is constantly in her way. They approach her with small

124

movements to position themselves for the throw, and she observes them through her terrified eyes, but there is a waiting quality about her, an absence of fury. The foal makes a pass toward her teats, and then, as though remembering, jerks up its head to watch the approaching men.

Now Gay halts. He is on one side of the mare, Guido in front of her. He tosses a noose behind her forefeet. Guido shouts and rushes at her face, and she backs into the noose which Gay pulls tight and, running behind her, yanks to trip her to her knees. Guido walks up beside her and pushes her and she falls to earth. Gay lashes her four feet together and drops his rope. Perce lets go his rope, draws up his knees, and rests his arms on them, looking into the distance. The foal walks to him and sniffs the ground a yard from his hand.

Gay takes out his cigarettes. Guido blows his nose. They are standing with their backs to the truck. The three sense Roslyn's eyes on them, and this knowledge is like a raging sea on which they ride, falling and rising within themselves, yet outwardly even more relaxed than if all were calm under them.

Gay inhales, and Perce knows now that he is gathering himself to turn about and go back to the truck to resume the roping of the remaining horses. The hurt is deepening in Gay's face and this sombre look of loss, this groping for his pride, is dangerous. 'We can rope the others on the way back. What you reckon this mare weighs?'

In Guido's eyes the emptiness is like a lake as he surveys the mare's body.

Now Perce slowly turns. Roslyn is looking skyward through the windshield and he knows she can hear this. 'There's hardly beer money in it for six, Gay.'

Gay's eyes remain defiantly fixed on Guido's profile as he waits for the figures and Perce says no more.

Now Guido looks at him. 'She might be six hundred pounds.'

Gay: 'The two browns be about four hundred, I'd say.'

Guido: 'Just about, ya.'

'Must be five hundred on the stallion, anyway.'

'A little lighter, I'd say. Call it nineteen hundred – two thousand pounds altogether.'

'How's that come out, now?'

Guido looks up in the air, figuring. 'Well, six cents a pound, that's –' He figures with silent, moving lips.

In the momentary silence they hear Roslyn's sobs fully pouring out of her. Gay and Guido keep their eyes on each other.

'Be about hundred and ten, hundred and twenty dollars, Gay.'

'Okay, how you want to cut it?'

'Anyway you like. . . . I'll take fifty for myself and the plane.'

'Okay. I guess I oughta have about forty for the truck and me. That'd give you twenty-five, Perce – that all right?'

Perce, staring at the mare, seems not to have heard.

'Perce?'

'You fellas take it. I just went along for the ride, anyway.'

Perce turns so sharply that the other two start. They see Roslyn walking. She is heading across the open lake bed.

'Roslyn!' Gay takes a step, and halts himself.

She has swerved about. Her shadow sketches toward them. Forty yards away, she screams, her body writhing, bending over as though to catapult her hatred.

'You liars! All of you!' Clenching her fists, she screams toward their faces: '*Liars!*'

Unnerved, Gay flinches.

'Man! Big man! You're only living when you can watch something die! Kill everything, that's all you want! Why don't you just kill yourselves and be happy?'

She runs toward them, but stops as though afraid, and

126

says directly toward Gay: 'You. With your God's country. Freedom!' She screams into his face: '*I hate you!*'

Unable to bear it, Gay mutters: 'We've had it now, Roslyn.'

'You sure did – more than *you'll* ever know. But you didn't want it. Nobody does. I pity you all.' Looking from one to another and beyond them to imagined others: 'You know everything except what it feels like to be alive. You're three dear, sweet dead men.'

'*She's crazy!*'

The weird resonance of Guido's cry turns them all to him. His eyes seem peeled back, fanatical, as though he had been seized from within by a pair of jaws which were devouring him as he stands there. His head and hands are shaking, he seems about to fly off the ground at her, and he goes on to his toes and down and up again. 'They're all crazy!' Now he moves away from Gay and back again, flinging his words toward Roslyn and beyond her toward the sky. 'You try not to believe it. Because you need them. You need them but they're crazy!' Tears spurt out of his eyes on to his cheeks but his ferocity is undiminished. 'You struggle, you build, you try, you turn yourself inside out for them, but nothing's ever enough! It's never a deal, something's always missing. It's gotta be perfect or they put the spurs to you! We ask them too much – and we tell them too little. I know – I got the marks!' He hits his chest with his fist, heaving for breath; the veins are standing out on his neck. Suddenly he looks down at the ground dizzily. He walks away and after a few yards he stops, throwing his head back, trying to catch his breath. She, exhausted, looking at nothing, bends over and seems to crumple, sitting on the ground, weeping quietly. Perce is looking at her through the corner of his eye. Gay walks around the prostrate mare, goes to the truck, and climbs on to the back. Perce goes over to her as though to help her up, but she gets to her feet, the talc caked on her jeans, and walks weakly toward the truck and gets in. Perce comes around and gets behind the wheel beside her. Now Guido returns, staring at the ground as though he had puzzled himself. He hops aboard. The truck starts away.

A blasted look is on Gay's face, as though he had been beaten in a fistfight in a cause he only half-believed. Squinting against the wind, his eyes hover on the high mountains, full of wish, almost expecting the sight of the hundreds, the full herds clambering into the open, the big horses and the sweet mares that gentled so quickly, the natural singlefooters, the smooth gallopers that just swept the ground under them, hardly touching it. . . .

Twelve

THE clinking of Guido's wrench is the only sound; all else is silence. He finishes screwing in his number-four spark plug, unclips a wire, lays his wrench on number five, and screws it out. His flashlight tucked under his arm illuminates his hands. He is whistling under his breath, strangly energized, glancing quickly now and then at the others and brimming over with some private hope of his own.

A few yards from him Gay stands staring out at the sky's starry arch, seeing nothing. A sense of mourning flows from his very stance; he has his hands on his hips as though he must support his back. He seems exhausted.

Squatting on his heels, Perce is motionless, smoking. He is ten yards from Gay, and yet he can feel his mood. Off to his left in the cab of the truck, Roslyn is resting her head against the doorframe, staring out over Perce's head toward a trussed horse lying on its side. As night deepens, only its darker mass is visible, and it never moves. Roslyn closes her eyes and seems to sleep.

Gay calls over to Guido: 'How long you gonna be with that?'

'No time at all now.' Guido's voice is high and crisp. He scrapes carbon from the plug's electrode and blows out the chips.

Roslyn sees Perce standing up. He walks over to her and stands. In the moonlight his face seems bonier and hard. His voice is close to a whisper, yet loud enough to avoid any air of conspiracy. 'I'd turn them loose. If you wanted.'

'No, don't fight.'

'He got himself up so high he can't get down now.' He looks over toward Gay, who is standing with his back to them. She feels in Perce his impatient love for the older man, and she knows his uncertainty about what to do.

'It doesn't matter, anyway.' She looks toward the trussed horse. 'It's all a joke – how easy they agree to die! It's like a dream, look, it doesn't even move. Is it sleeping?'

'Might be, sure.'

'Couldn't they leave the colt here?'

'Wouldn't stay. Follow the truck right into town. Probably drop on the way in.'

He turns and leans against the door, looking with her toward the dark shape of the trussed horse. 'I wish I'd met you a long time ago. Save me a lot of broken bones.'

She turns to him, then reaches out and touches his arm.

He faces her. 'I'd just about gave up – expectin' anything.' He comes in closer to her, taking a breath. 'I'd cut them loose for you.'

They hear Guido's voice and turn quickly, seeing Gay going to him at the engine. Guido hands him the flashlight, which he shines on a spark plug in Guido's hand. Holding it up close to his eyes, Guido passes a feeler gauge between the electrode and the ground pin, then knocks the ground pin to lessen the gap and measures it again. They can hear his voice and his quiet laugh.

Guido: 'Buck up, boy. Before you know it you'll be up to your neck in girls again.'

Gay is annoyed, wanting to be off as quickly as possible.

But Guido goes on: 'I just been thinking . . . I don't know how we got so stupid. The world's full of mountains . . . Colorado, Montana, Canada, even Mexico; and where there's mountains there's *got* to be horses. Probably we couldn't clean them all out till we're too stiff to walk. Now if we worked a while, and I'd even sell my house – I don't know what I was keepin' it for anyway – and put everything into a good plane . . . we could get this thing on a business basis.'

Gay shifts on to one hip, a deepening disgust and anger rising into his face.

Guido: 'Why, we never even watered the horses before we weighted them in! We could put fifty pounds on just these five if we let them drink. We just been foolin' around with it.'

Impatiently indicating for him to resume working on the spark plug, Gay hardly moves his lips. 'I want to get out of here, come on.'

As he screws the spark plug into the engine, Guido's confidence seems to flow. 'With a good plane we could fly into Reno from anywhere – check in at the Mapes, have us a time, and off we go again! Boy, we wouldn't need anybody in this world!' He has taken the flashlight, and waits for Gay's reply.

Gay's face is flushed as though he were exerting himself to lift something. At last he bursts out in a pained voice: 'Why don't you shut up, Guido?' Guido straightens in shock at the rumble of disgust he hears. 'Just shut up, will you?'

But Guido smiles directly into Gay's threatening gaze. 'Meet you at the dealer's in the morning; get his winch truck if we're early. Six o'clock, okay?'

Gay's non-reply is his agreement, and Guido moves away along the wing, goes to the cockpit, and climbs in. Gay stands before the propeller. 'Okay, give her a twist – switch off!'

For a moment Gay seems not to have heard. His eyes are sightless, inward-looking. Roslyn and Perce can see him standing there.

'Turn her over, boy, huh?'

Gay faces the plane, reaches up, turns the propeller. The engine clicks like a clock being wound. Gay seems to be moving in slow motion, pulling the blade down, then gradually raising his arms and pulling it down again, priming the cylinders.

Perce walks along the length of the truck and Roslyn turns to watch him. He disappears around the back of it. She looks at the plane again.

Guido: 'Okay! Switch on!'

Gay positions himself more carefully. The propeller is horizontal. He lays both hands on the blade, swings his right leg across his left, and quickly pulls and hops away as the engine clatters up to a puffing roar. He walks backward along the wing until he clears it. Guido motions from the cockpit for him to watch out for the dog, which is still tied to a stake under the wing. Gay motions for Guido to take off.

The engine's roar increases and the propeller becomes a wheel in the moonlight. The plane bucks forward and back against the grip of the wheel brakes as Guido warms the engine. In the cockpit Guido is focusing the flashlight on his gauges. Now the engine roars up to its peak.

Roslyn turns quickly, seeing Perce getting in behind the wheel beside her. He starts the truck engine. She looks through the windshield toward Gay, who is now holding the dog's body down as the wing of the plane passes over it. The truck is suddenly in motion as the plane taxis away in the direction of the moon. She involuntarily grabs Perce's arm to stop him, but he now switches on the headlights and swerves the truck toward the trussed horse. Roslyn leans out the window and sees the plane taxiing off into the darkness, and Gay turning from it and finding the truck gone. He swings about, looks toward her, and starts to run. The truck's brakes squeal and it skids to a halt beside the trussed horse; Perce leaps out and runs to it, with an open clasp-knife in his hand. He leans over the horse's belly and cuts the rope around its hooves, and it starts scrambling to stand up. He rushes to the tyre and cuts the rope; the horse, on its feet, trots away for a few yards and stands stiffly. Perce starts to run after it and shoo it off but he sees Gay bearing down on him and hears his roaring voice. He jumps into the truck, grinds it into gear, and jams the gas pedal to the floor. The wheels spin for an instant and it jerks and roars away.

A wordless command bellows from Gay's furious face. He rushes toward the horse, which now trots, not very fast. The rope is trailing from its neck and he reaches down for it, but the animal's sense of him speeds it into a canter. Gay lunges for the rope and falls, and the horse clatters off into the darkness. He gets to his feet, turns in a circle. The headlights of the truck are impossibly distant now. He runs toward them. Tears are on his cheeks and angry calls come from his throat, but more than anger is his clear frustration, as though above all his hand had been forced from its grip on his life and he had been made smaller.

The truck halts beside another horse. Perce leaps out, cuts it loose, and rushes back into the truck and speeds it away. A wave of guilt passes over Roslyn's face now. She scans the lake bed for a sign of Gay. In her uncertainty she turns to Perce. His mildness has vanished and he seems inspired, a wild, rebellious joy on his face.

Guido has taxied close to the edge of the lake bed. For a moment he sits slumped on the torn cushions, staring out at nothing, wanting the engine's roar to enter and overwhelm his mind. He cuts the throttle; the plane slows, and he turns it about to face the wind. Far across the lake bed the mountain face gleams in the moonlight as though covered with snow; the white clay stretching away before him is luminescent with a greenish silvery light that does not brighten the air but clings to the ground like a heavy gas. He has nowhere to go and no reason to move; the threat of total emptiness angers him. He guns the engine and the plane hurries. As he starts to press the stick forward to raise the tail and climb, his eye catches the truck's moving headlights; but he realizes that,

oddly, it is not moving toward the sage desert and the home-
ward direction. Airborne, he flattens the trajectory of the
plane, banks sharply, leans out the side of the cockpit a man's
height above the earth. A horse is just crossing the headlight
beams below – a horse running free. He pushes the stick
forward, settling himself to watch the ground coming up
beneath him, striving to remember where each horse was
tethered, envisioning the crash should he hit one as he comes
in to land.

A mile away the headlight beams pick up the stallion's form.
Roslyn looks out and as it nears she cries out: 'Oh, Perce!
I don't know!' He glances at her surprised, perplexed, and
brakes the truck.

The trussed stallion, ears cocked to the truck's sound,
arches up his head. Perce runs to the tyre. The stallion yanks
it as he saws the rope. Roslyn runs out of the cab, glancing
about guiltily for a sign of Gay. Suddenly the rope parts. The
stallion, free, kicks up his rear legs, rushes past them, and turns
about. Perce pulls her out of the way and yells wordlessly to
scare off the beast. Before the reality of the freed stallion,
Roslyn feels an ecstatic, terrified conviction. Almost unaware
of her own voice, she cries out: 'Go! Go home! Go home!'

Perce runs toward the stallion, which turns and gallops
away, his neck rope trailing. Breathless, they watch him for a
moment, then run to the truck. Roslyn gets into the cab.
Perce halts, scanning the glowing lake bed, calculates the
location of the two remaining horses, and hurries into the
truck.

From the open cockpit of the taxiing plane Guido method-
ically keeps turning his eyes across the breadth of the lake
bed, swinging the plane in wide arcs. Now two specs of light
move very far away. He guns the plane toward them.

The headlights are larger in Gay's eyes. He has changed
direction with their every movement, and now, impossibly

134

distant, he stills runs mechanically, anaesthetized by his impotence. A tacking sound stops him instantly.

Trying to control his wheezing breath, wiping sweat from his eyes, he turns about slowly, listening. The moon is glowing and the lake bed seems bright, but night begins a few inches off the ground. His heart is surging in his chest, a pulse beating in his eyes. Again a shadow moves. He widens his eyes to be sure. He slowly sits down on his heels and makes himself small. A shadow moves again. He senses its direction now; surprisingly, it is not headed for the mountains. He turns toward the centre of the lake bed. Gradually his eyes perceive the black forms of the mare and colt far off under the moon. Now he turns back toward the moving form. The tacking sound is closer now.

Silently he rises and moves toward the trussed mare, keeping his mouth wide open to let his breath escape without sound. He sees the colt getting to its feet now and lengthens his steps, keeping his head down. He halts at the sudden jagged sound of the mare's snickering. Off to his left, the stallion's form moves closer to her, and it stands over her trussed form. Gay sees its neck stretching down to her. He is moving again, crouching low, and now he runs. The stallion's head shoots up and it backs and stands, listening. The moon makes a yellow disc of one eye as Gay comes in from the side and grasps its neck rope in both gloved hands. The horse bares its teeth and gouges for his shoulder, and he slips his hands farther down along the rope, murmuring to it, but it suddenly swerves and gallops. Gay wraps the rope around his arm and runs behind, trying to dig in his heels. A quick burst of force yanks him about and he falls. He is being dragged on his side, the talc blinding him. The rope suddenly slackens; he scrambles to his feet and the shoulder of the horse hits the side of his head as it gallops past, and he is pulled to the ground again. He sits up, swinging his boots around in front of him, seeking the clay with his heels. The stallion coughs and wheels, and for a moment stands facing him where he sits. The noose, he knows, is not tight enough to make it wheeze as it does, and he again wraps the rope around his arm, digging his heels in and preparing in his mind to roll away if it should charge him there. The stallion backs, experimentally it seems, testing his weight on the rope.

Gay starts sidling toward the mare. She is a length away. He reaches her without taking his eyes from the stallion, and feels with his elbow for the shape of her, trying to sense how far he must move to reach her neck rope and the tyre. At his touch she shudders; he feels her quarter, and sidles so that she is between him and the stallion, which is restive on its hooves but not pulling hard any more. Gay gets his heels under him and creeps sideways toward the mare's neck. Now he has her neck rope under his arm. He becomes still. He will have to unwrap the rope to tie it to the mare's noose.

The stallion eyes him, gasping. Gay murmurs to him across the mare's neck: 'Whoa now, whoa now, whoa now . . .' He begins to unwrap his arm, always keeping both hands around the rope. The stallion's head rises, and Gay stops moving. He knows the movement of the rope is vibrating into the stallion's body and can set him going again. After a moment, he again moves his arm to uncoil the rope. The mare suddenly blows out a high snicker, and the stallion flings its head into the air; Gay is yanked toward him over the mare's body. He goes with the force and lets it carry him to his feet; he leaps for the stallion's neck to pull the noose tight with both hands and the animal gallops, kicking out its hind legs, but Gay can feel it trembling and its power weakening. He hangs from the noose, pulling it down with all his force, the backs of his thighs being pounded by the horse's knees.

The stallion halts. Gay hangs his full weight from the tightening noose. The stallion's neck lowers and his shaking knees start to buckle. Gay yanks again, a short scream escaping his throat as a broken, thin cry vibrates in the stallion's head.

Gay hears an engine. He yanks again, raising his feet off the ground, pulling the stallion's head lower. The headlight beams hit his face and burn his eyes. He hears the brakes squealing and the doors opening.

On both Roslyn's and Perce's faces is a look of near awe. The stallion is motionless, groaning against the asphyxiating noose. And yet between it and Gay hanging from its neck there is a strange relation, an aura of understanding; it is as though the vanquished beast belonged to Gay now, however this came to be, and that it knew this even as it would not come to earth.

Perce picks up the rope end and lashes it to the truck bumper. 'Okay, let him go!'

Gay springs away from the horse, which tucks in its head and walks slowly and halts.

Swaying on his feet, Gay moves to the truck and lies over the hood, his arms outstretched.

He slowly opens his cramped hands. Roslyn does not approach him. She watches him from her distance, as Perce does, and she seems to soften under the power of his struggle. A wonder is rising in her eyes. She takes a step toward him, but Perce reaches out quickly and stops her. She sees fear in Perce's face, and she becomes afraid not so much of Gay's violence as of having done a thing which now she cannot comprehend.

The plane engine is heard, and in a moment it comes to halt nearby. The engine is cut; Guido leaps out and runs toward Gay. Seeing him heaving for breath and the stallion tied, he laughs toward Perce and bends over Gay to give him a quick hug.

'You held him! Good boy! We'll get them all back tomorrow! Get your wind now, just get your wind now. . . .' He warmly pats Gay's back.

Gay is still sucking air, his trunk bent over the truck hood, his eyes staring at the stallion. Guido grips his shoulder. 'Don't you worry, boy – we ain't through here. Not by a long shot! We're only starting! I'll go up to Thighbone Mountain with you – hear? There's five thousand dollars up there, but we gotta work at it. We'll *horseback* in up there! And there's more, there's more – but we gotta work at it! 'Cause we don't need nobody in this world, Gay – and I guess you know it now, don't you?' Toward Roslyn: 'To hell with them all!'

Gay, oblivious of Guido, is staring at the mustang, his cheek pressed against the truck hood. His eyes seem to be peering toward a far point, and about him is a stillness, as though he were alone here. He straightens, slipping a hand into his pocket.

Guido reaches to him: 'Come on, I'll fly you back. They can take the –' He breaks off, seeing a clasp-knife opening in Gay's hand. When he looks again into his face he sees tears in his eyes, and he is bewildered and, for the moment, silent.

Gay walks straight at him as though he did not see him, and Guido, stepping out of his path, asks: 'What are – ?' But Gay has bent to the rope at the bumper and is cutting it, his hand shaking. Guido grabs at his hand and holds it, and understands enough to raise a panic in his eyes as he stands pressed close to his friend. Gay's caked lips move; in a cracked whisper, looking into Guido's face but blind to him: 'It's all finished.'

'What the hell'd you catch him for?'

'Just . . . done it. Don't like nobody makin' up my mind for me, that's all.'

A tremor seems to go through his body, and his brows tense together as though he would weep in anger. He weakly presses Guido to move aside, but Guido holds his wrist.

'I'll go with you to Thighbone!'

Gay shakes his head. He looks beyond Guido to the darkened hills, and anger hardens his face and straightens him. 'God damn them all! They changed it. Changed it all around. They smeared it all over with blood, turned it into shit and money just like everything else. You know that. I know that. It's just ropin' a dream now.' He slips his wrist out of Guido's grasp. 'Find some other way to know you're alive . . . if they got another way, any more.' He turns to the rope and leans his weight on the knife; the rope, cut, falls to the ground.

For a moment, the stallion does not move. With the pressure off the noose it stretches its neck and, taking a step to the side, almost stumbles to the ground, rights itself, and walks. Then it halts, stands unsteadily, and goes away. Gay walks over to the mare and cuts her hoof ropes and then the rope to the tyre; she weightily clambers up and trots away, the foal following with its nose in her flying tail.

The four stand listening to the fading sound of the hooves. Gay, closing his knife and slipping it into his pocket, walks from Guido, looking at no one, absorbed in himself.

Their eyes follow him as he goes by and gets into the truck behind the wheel, exhausted, silent. For a moment he stares ahead through the windshield. Roslyn is on the opposite side of the truck now, looking across the empty seat at him. In this moment it is unknown what he will do, and she does not move. He turns to her, his loneliness in his eyes. 'Drive you back . . . if you want.'

Hesitant and afraid of him still, she gets into the seat, but not close to him. Her open stare is full of his pain and his loss.

Perce has come up to her window. 'I'm pleased to have met you, Roslyn.'

Roslyn: 'Don't hurt yourself any more, will you?'

He thanks her with his eyes. 'If you ever feel like droppin' a card, my address is just Black River . . . California.'

Gay starts the engine and turns to Guido, who is on his side of the truck. 'See you around. Give you a call in a couple days.'

Guido, his eyes sharpened with resentment, laughs. 'Where'll you be? Some gas station, polishing windshields?'

'You got me there, Pilot.' Gay turns forward and starts the truck rolling.

Guido jumps on to the running-board, laughing and yelling at him: 'Or making change in the supermarket!'

Guido jumps off, and makes a megaphone of his hands, furiously calling: 'Try the laundromat – they might need a fella to load the machines!'

But the truck is moving away, and his need is wide; he cries out, his fist in the air: 'Gay! Where you goin'?'

He has come to a halt, angry and lost. Perce stands there, tears flowing into his eyes.

Gay drives in silence, exhausted. Roslyn is still a distance from him on the seat. Now she turns to him, not knowing his feeling. They seem like strangers for a moment.

'I'll leave tomorrow.' She is asking, but he remains silent. 'Okay?' He drives on. 'You'll never believe it, but I didn't mean to harm you. . . . I honour you. You're a brave man.'

He is silent.

'You don't like me any more. Do you?'

Now she turns forward. Her voice wavers. Everything seems to be moving away from her.

'But you know something? For a minute, when those horses galloped away, it was almost like I gave them back their life. And all of a sudden I got a feeling – it's crazy! – I suddenly thought, "He must love me, or how would I dare do this?" Because I always just ran away when I couldn't stand it. Gay – for a minute you made me not afraid. And it was like my life flew into my body. For the first time.'

He sees the dog in the headlight beams, tied to one of the stakes, and halts the truck.

She opens her door, but turns back to him as though she cannot leave. And suddenly she cries out, desperately: 'Oh, Gay, what is there? Do you know? What is there that stays?'

He turns to her for the first time. There are tears in his eyes.

He draws her to him and kisses her. She is weeping with joy, trying to see through his eyes into him.

Gay: 'God knows. Everything I ever see was comin' or goin' away. Same as you. Maybe the only thing is . . . the knowin'. 'Cause I know you now, Roslyn, I do know you. Maybe that's all the peace there is or can be. I never bothered to battle a woman before. And it was peaceful, but a lot like huggin' the air. This time, I thought I'd lay my hand on the air again – but it feels like I touched the whole world. I bless you, girl.'

She flies to his face, kissing him passionately. The dog barks outside. She runs out of the cab to it, and it greets her joyfully. She unties it and claps her hands to make it follow. The dog leaps on to the truck bed and she re-enters the cab, her face infused with an overflowing love. He starts the truck and they drive. Suddenly, with the quick rapture of her vision: 'If . . . if we weren't afraid! Gay? And there could be a child. And we could make it brave. One person in the world who would be brave from the beginning! I was scared to last night. But I'm not so much now. Are you?'

He clasps her close to his hip. He drives. The love between them is viable, holding them a little above the earth. The headlights pick up clumps of sage now, and the ride is bumpy.

Roslyn: 'How do your find you way back in the dark?'

Gay nods, indicating the sky before them: 'Just head for that big star straight on. The highway's under it; take us right home.'

She raises her eyes to the star through the streaks and dust of the windshield. The sound of Guido's plane roars in and away, invisible overhead. The truck's headlights gradually disappear, and with them all sound. Now there is only the sky full of stars, and absolute silence.

4

SOME RECENT PENGUIN FICTION

—

WILLIAM COOPER · *Scenes from Provincial Life*
'Often hilariously funny, always true' – C. P. Snow (1527)*

ANGUS WILSON · *The Middle Age of Mrs Eliot*
'Towers above the fiction of a decade' – *Daily Telegraph* (1502)*

C. P. SNOW · *The Conscience of the Rich*
A novel of conflict in Anglo-Jewish society (1526)*

FREDERICK BUECHNER · *The Return of Ansel Gibbs*
'Weird, compelling ... an experience to read' – *Time and Tide*
(1559)†

A. E. ELLIS · *The Rack*
Love and pain in a French T.B. sanatorium (1545)*

JOHN MASTERS · *Far, Far the Mountain Peak*
A masterly study of a cold and ruthless climber (1543)†

* NOT FOR SALE IN THE U.S.A.
† NOT FOR SALE IN THE U.S.A. OR CANADA

MODERN CONTINENTAL WRITERS

—

Sartre and Camus from France, Moravia from Italy, Brecht from Germany – these are just a few of the exciting modern writers on the Penguin list. Together with the more established names of Thomas Mann, Marcel Proust, Franz Kafka, and many others, they form an impressive selection of European writers.

Works by the following authors are available in Penguins:

JEAN ANOUILH · ISAAC BABEL

UGO BETTI · BERTOLT BRECHT

GIL BUHET · ALBERT CAMUS

GABRIEL CHEVALLIER · COLETTE

PIERRE DANINOS · ANTOINE DE SAINT-EXUPÉRY

MAX FRISCH · ROMAIN GARY

ANDRÉ GIDE · JAROSLAV HAŠEK

FRANZ KAFKA · ANDRÉ MALRAUX

THOMAS MANN · FRANÇOIS MAURIAC · ALBERTO MORAVIA

ROBERT MUSIL · BORIS PASTERNAK

LUIGI PIRANDELLO · MARCEL PROUST

FRANÇOISE SAGAN · JEAN-PAUL SARTRE

GEORGES SIMENON · ROGER VAILLAND

MARGUERITE YOURCENAR